S0-AFH-243

BUSHWHACKER SURPRISE

Fargo waited. He knew this new game. The shooter in the brush had been hit once or twice, or he was playing possum and not wounded at all, just waiting for his chance.

Fargo moved silently up the woods beside the gully where it narrowed. Just around a slight curve where he couldn't see the shooter's position, Fargo crossed the gully. Then he began to move quietly through the light brush and gum and maple trees.

To cover fifty yards took several cautious minutes. When he figured he was twenty yards from the gunman, he stopped and listened. He soon heard a soft mumbling of words ahead. The man might have taken a bullet in a leg so he couldn't move.

Fargo held his cocked Colt in his right hand as he crawled forward without a whisper of a leaf. Another ten feet and Fargo could see him. He had his hat off, one arm was bloody, and his leg was twisted unnaturally under him. He leaned back against a gum tree, his face showing his pain.

Fargo fired one shot an inch over the man's head. The sound of the round going off in the brush was twice as loud as usual. The bushwhacker jumped; then his hand went down toward his revolver.

"Don't touch it or you're dead," Fargo thundered.

THE
TRAILSMAN
#233

MISSOURI
MAYHEM

by

Jon Sharpe

A SIGNET BOOK

SIGNET
Published by New American Library, a division of
Penguin Putnam Inc., 375 Hudson Street,
New York, New York 10014, U.S.A.
Penguin Books Ltd, 27 Wrights Lane,
London W8 5TZ, England
Penguin Books Australia Ltd, Ringwood,
Victoria, Australia
Penguin Books Canada Ltd, 10 Alcorn Avenue,
Toronto, Ontario, Canada M4V 3B2
Penguin Books (N.Z.) Ltd, 182–190 Wairau Road,
Auckland 10, New Zealand

Penguin Books Ltd, Registered Offices:
Harmondsworth, Middlesex, England

First published by Signet, an imprint of New American Library,
a division of Penguin Putnam Inc.

First Printing, March 2001
10 9 8 7 6 5 4 3 2 1

Copyright © Jon Sharpe, 2001

All rights reserved

The first chapter of this book originally appeared in *Pacific Phantoms*,
the two hundred thirty-second volume in this series.

Ⓙ REGISTERED TRADEMARK—MARCA REGISTRADA

Printed in the United States of America

Without limiting the rights under copyright reserved above, no part of this
publication may be reproduced, stored in or introduced into a retrieval system, or
transmitted, in any form, or by any means (electronic, mechanical, photocopying,
recording, or otherwise), without the prior written permission of both the copyright
owner and the above publisher of this book.

PUBLISHER'S NOTE
This is a work of fiction. Names, characters, places, and incidents either are the
product of the author's imagination or are used fictitiously, and any resemblance to
actual persons, living or dead, events, or locales is entirely coincidental.

BOOKS ARE AVAILABLE AT QUANTITY DISCOUNTS WHEN USED TO PROMOTE PRODUCTS OR
SERVICES. FOR INFORMATION PLEASE WRITE TO PREMIUM MARKETING DIVISION, PENGUIN
PUTNAM INC., 375 HUDSON STREET, NEW YORK, NEW YORK 10014.

If you purchased this book without a cover you should be aware that this book is
stolen property. It was reported as "unsold and destroyed" to the publisher and neither
the author nor the publisher has received any payment for this "stripped book."

The Trailsman

Beginnings . . . they bend the tree and they mark the man. Skye Fargo was born when he was eighteen. Terror was his midwife, vengeance his first cry. Killing spawned Skye Fargo, ruthless, cold-blooded murder. Out of the acrid smoke of gunpowder still hanging in the air, he rose, cried out a promise never forgotten.

The Trailsman they began to call him all across the West: searcher, scout, hunter, the man who could see where others only looked, his skills for hire but not his soul, the man who lived each day to the fullest, yet trailed each tomorrow. Skye Fargo, the Trailsman, the seeker who could take the wildness of a land and the wanting of a woman and make them his own.

Western Missouri, 1861—near the small town of Plainview, where the men lived hard and the women even harder, and where turning your back on your kin could earn you a deadly bullet.

1

Skye Fargo lounged on the soft bed, a welcome change after two weeks on the trail. He reached over and kissed the striking brunette who lay beside him. Then he sipped from a glass of whiskey and chuckled. This was the life. What the hell, it was the railroad's money. They had been plagued by a series of six brazen train robberies, and they had hired him, at a hefty sum, to help stop them.

When Fargo had checked his mail drop two weeks ago, there had been an urgent request to contact the Missouri & Illinois Central Railroad main office in St. Louis. He had done so from the nearest telegraph and had been hired by a return wire at one and a half times his usual daily fee.

Here he sat in Plainview, almost at the end of the Missouri & Illinois Central Railroad line, waiting for something to happen. He'd been here a week with no action. The railroad could afford it, even a small line like the M&I.

He had found the lady lying beside him crying outside the telegraph office his second day in town. He had spoken to her, eventually buying her a cup of tea, and then talking most of the afternoon in the Farm Home Café.

Her name was Betty, and she had just discovered by wire that her betrothed had decided to call off the wedding and stay in St. Louis, where he had gone to visit his family. She was crushed. Fargo charmed her with the tea and later bought her dinner at the same café.

She had taken a room at the least expensive hotel in the small town, and planned on staying only two nights until her fiancé came back. Fargo had been with her since that first dinner.

He looked down at Betty. She had long, gently curling hair, as black as a crow's wing. Serious green eyes glowed under heavy brows, flanking a delicate nose. She had a round face that was more striking than beautiful. Firm shoulders over ample breasts, with large pink circles and brown nipples, still aroused him. She had a generous waist tapering to strong legs and a dense triangle of dark hair. She pushed delightfully against him.

"Again, Fargo. It's so good in the morning."

Fargo put down the glass and moved over her.

A knock came on the door at the same time. Fargo and Betty looked at each other. The knock sounded again, more impatient. After a pause someone shouted.

"Fargo, if you're in there, the district manager wants to see you pronto in his office. He said that means right now, dammit."

"Yeah, I'm coming," Fargo said. He pushed off the bed and put on his buckskins. They made him stand out in this citified town. But he kept wearing them, because they were efficient clothes—in or out of the wilderness. Besides, they reinforced his image and reputation as the best trailsman in the West.

When he was dressed, he bent and kissed both of Betty's still throbbing nipples. "Keep that idea in mind. I'll be back as soon as I can make it."

Five minutes later in the train station, Fargo pushed through the door to the Missouri & Illinois Central Railroad's office and looked at Durward Neville, the road's district manager.

"You called?" Fargo asked. Neville was engrossed in some papers on his desk. He looked up with nervous light blue eyes and a thin face that had a mole high on his left cheek. He rubbed it without realizing it.

"Yes, Fargo. We have something that might interest you. Back down the line near St. Louis we had an attempted rob-

2

bery. Two gunmen tried to get into the Railway Express car, but couldn't because there's no door on either end of the car. So they robbed the passengers in five coaches, and jumped off the train when the conductor got out of his ropes and pulled the emergency stop signal. Never found either of the robbers. Nobody shot or hurt. In fact, no shots were fired. You want to go back down the line about eighty miles and check it out?"

"No. Their trail would be a day old or more before I could get there. Not a chance I could find even where they left the train unless someone spotted a mile marker or some house or farm. Chances of that are zero. I'll go if you order me back there, but I can tell you right now, it would be a waste of time."

"That's what we're paying you for, to track these people whether you waste time or not." Neville rubbed the balding top of his head, brought down his hand, and wiped it on his pants. Beads of sweat immediately returned to his forehead. "Damn, damn, damn. Why do I have to make the decisions that the directors always yell about?"

"You're the district manager," Fargo said.

Neville closed his eyes and gave a long sigh. "An easy job out there thirty miles from the end of the tracks. Nothing to it, they told me. A spot to climb up the corporate advancement ladder in M&I Central." He shook his head. "Hate to say it, but you're right. Too far, too late. They have a rail detective in St. Louis who's lots closer. I'll suggest that they send him."

"Good decision," Fargo said. "Anything else?"

"I've got money to fund you for three weeks, Fargo. There was no action the first week. I'm hoping that your being here might scare off the robbers. Worked last year when we advertised that a Pinkerton detective would be riding every train. Trouble was, the Pinks cost us as much as the robbers had been stealing from us."

When Fargo walked back to the Plains Hotel and up to the second-story room, he found Betty had dressed. The

3

low-cut white blouse showed an inch of cleavage and was tightly filled. Fargo brushed her lips with his quickly, bent and kissed her bosom, then announced it was time for lunch.

"I thought you might not come back."

"Some trouble down the line toward St. Louis. Not my territory. But if something happens around here, you won't see me for a spell."

In the café, they sat down to enjoy a dinner of roast beef with mashed potatoes, gravy, and three vegetables. Betty put it all away easily, and they even had room afterward for pie with whipped cream topping for dessert.

As they walked back through the cool May evening air to the hotel, Fargo grinned into the night. This was great duty when you could get it. Still he was afraid that it wouldn't last long.

2

The dark stink of fear gushed over him like a polluted river. Wendell Mannington stared at the two outlaws, especially the one holding the six-gun aimed at his belly from three feet away. He remembered being this terrified only twice before. Once in a sweeping green field at Gettysburg, when horror almost overwhelmed him as men on all sides were falling like stalks of wheat under the scythe of the Yankee minie balls.

The second time was when he was a fireman and rode old Engine 421 off the tracks, through a wooden trestle, and down two hundred feet into Jensen Canyon.

"Old man, I'm a'talkin' to ya," the gunman said. He was in his twenties, tall, dressed as a working cowboy but without the usual outdoors tan. He held a big .45 in his hand and seemed eager to use it. "I ask if ya wanted ta get your damned head blowed off, or you gonna unlock the door into the next car."

Conductor Mannington stared hard at him. "Can't. Ain't no door on the end of the car. Look, no keyhole. That's the Railway Express Car. It's built that way. Door that was there been sealed shut. Only doors that open are on the sides of the car."

"The hell you say." The tall gunman frowned. He wiped sweat off his forehead, pushing back locks of red hair. His green eyes widened, showing too much white, then he blinked. He snorted and motioned to his cohort beside him.

"Your job then, buddy. Get it done. We runnin' out of time."

The pair had come out of the passenger coach and confronted the forty-nine-year-old trainman two minutes ago in the small connector space between the rail cars.

"My name's Red Plimpton, and I want y'all to remember me," the tall gunman said. "I rob trains." He grinned, twisted his face into a sardonic smile, then lowered his revolver's muzzle and shot the conductor in the right thigh.

Conductor Mannington jolted backward from the force of the big .45 slug and slammed against the door to the passenger car. A wail of pain surged through his clenched teeth. Then he slid to the floor, his hands gripping the two gashes in his leg where the big lead slug had entered and then ripped out the other side.

The noise of the shot going off in the confined space sounded like a close lightning strike. With the sudden explosive noise, Mannington couldn't even hear the clicking of the wheels on the rail joints. He blinked back tears as the searing pain in his leg billowed into his brain. It was a fuzzy picture he saw in front of him across the car connector.

The second robber, Phil Kitts, worked on the end of the Express car. He was a head shorter than his partner, had a paunch and a holstered revolver. He pulled a four-inch-square box from his shoulder bag, inserted a six-inch fuse, and wedged the bomb against the Express car's rear sealed door.

A black powder bomb, the conductor decided. He wiped his hand over his face, smearing it with blood from his leg. Too much blood. He needed to stop it. He edged toward the passenger car door. That much black powder would mean a thunderous explosion and could kill him. The outlaw lit the six-inch fuse and watched it burn a moment. Then both robbers hurried past him to the passenger-side door, pushed through it, and pulled the door tightly shut.

Conductor Mannington knew exactly what would happen. He tried to stand but realized he couldn't. He tried to get the passenger-coach door open, but from where he lay on the floor, the handle was too far over his head. He knew he didn't have time to struggle up and pull out the fuse. He had to get away from the blast.

Stretching upward to grasp the door handle, he forgot and put weight on his right leg and brayed in pain as the wound angrily responded. He groaned and fell back to the floor, dizzy from the effort. How could he get away from the blast? He looked around the area and saw a spot that might be safe. It was a curved steel section of the car that joined with the next one and would provide a small buffer between him and the explosives. He looked at the bomb and saw the fuse burning closer to the powder.

Mannington rolled toward the safe zone, groaning as he turned over on his right leg. The conductor wedged tightly against the side of the car so the protective steel was between him and the powder. At the last moment, he curled into a ball, with his hands holding the back of his head and his arms over his face. He pressed his arms hard against the side of the passenger car and waited.

The roar came as loud as a high-balling freight blasting head-on into a passenger train. He felt a gigantic fist pound him hard against the brutally solid steel. The small space between the two cars instantly filled with smoke and fumes. The conductor choked and coughed from the acrid gases until the wind whipped some of them away. The blast had deafened him. All he could do was watch through the smoke as the passenger-car door jolted open. Before the conductor could sit up, the two gunmen ran through the connector.

"Oh, yeah, just right," the tall man shouted. The conductor didn't hear the words, but stared past the outlaws and saw the solid steel door to the Express car hanging only by the top hinge. He saw the robbers push the door aside and slide through the opening.

The conductor rolled over and caught the open passenger-car door before it swung shut after the outlaws. He held it open and crawled through into the coach. The people in the seats yelled and screamed. A woman fainted. A dozen voices called, but he still couldn't hear. He pointed at his ears and shook his head.

He tried to stand up, but fell half into a seat. He rested there a moment before he pushed up to his feet. He looked at the woman sitting in the window seat.

"Madam, we're being robbed," he said, not hearing himself. "Please reach up and pull the emergency cord."

The woman hesitated, said something he couldn't hear. Conductor Mannington repeated his request. The woman pulled the cord.

The train at once began to slow. He began to hear again. It was the welcome screech from the wheels on the rails as the brakes came on.

"What the hell happened up there?"

"Was that a bomb blast?"

"Those two guys with guns, they robbing the train?"

Mannington ignored the passengers' voices.

"Pull the cord again," the conductor told the woman. She did. Far ahead, the engineer heard the second signal, pulled the throttle back all the way, and continued the emergency braking process. From thirty-five miles an hour, it would take a half mile to stop the train with the long string of cars.

As the conductor slid into a seat, the two outlaws in the Railway Express car eyed their prize.

Plimpton had charged through the sagging door first, his .45 in hand. Through the still heavy smoke he saw a trainman stagger toward him, his special Railway Express cap tilted crazily to one side. To Plimpton he looked dazed. The agent blinked, then feebly held up one hand at the two outlaws in protest.

"You can't—"

Plimpton shot the agent twice in the chest and watched

him jolt backward against a rack of mail sacks, then topple to the floor.

"Work fast, dammit, Kitts, we don't got much time," the redhead shouted. "I'll look for the registered mail sacks. You blow the safe like we planned."

Kitts ran to the Railway Express safe, built solidly into the side frame of the car. He produced another small box of black powder, taping it firmly to the safe door with white medical tape. He cut a three-inch fuse and inserted it into the box of powder. As soon as he lit the fuse, the two robbers charged away from it to the front of the car, behind some heavy wooden boxes of freight.

The bomb exploded less than five seconds later. In the enclosed car, the roar was louder this time. Neither of the men could hear for a minute. They motioned to each other as they had planned. Kitts pulled open the safe door and both men grinned. They stepped over the dead agent, then worked quickly.

"Oh yeah, bank notes, federal money. We're in luck," the redhead shouted in glee. Part of his hearing was back. He fell sideways as the train suddenly began to slow. They could hear the screech of brakes.

"Guess our friend the conductor pulled the emergency cord the way we hoped he would," Plimpton said. "Hurry now." He took out two ten-pound gold bars from the safe, then the four familiar taped green cardboard boxes he knew contained freshly printed twenty-dollar bills. He stuffed it all into a canvas bag and hefted it. "Not too heavy. You check the marker?" Plimpton asked.

"Damn right. Think this is the first train I've robbed? We meet our man with the horses just past the eighty-seventh marker." Kitts unlocked and pushed open the large sliding side door so they could see the country. "We should spot our marker soon. The horse man should find us before we have to walk ten minutes."

"Greenbacks and gold," Plimpton said with satisfaction.

"That's a bonus. Hey, we might get paid more. You find that damn registered mail bag?"

"Two of them," Kitt said. "So we take them both. Can't tell which one has the goods Dutch is hunting for."

The train slowed more.

"Time to get the hell out of here," Plimpton said. They watched out the door, saw mile marker eighty-seven flash past. The train had slowed to twenty miles an hour. They threw the canvas bags and the mail sacks out the door and jumped.

Both men rolled down a small bank. Plimpton hit a rock and scraped his knee and limped as they scrambled into a green patch of brush and small hardwood trees. They hid twenty yards from the tracks and watched the rest of the train coast past. When it was well beyond them, they grabbed the two canvas bags and the two mail sacks, and hurried away.

A few seconds later they heard the train grind to a stop a hundred yards up the tracks. The fireman ran back, and the first passengers came off the car. The fireman found the conductor in the passenger's seat and tied a makeshift bandage around his bleeding right leg.

"Express car," Mannington brayed. "They blew the door and robbed the Express car. Take my telegraph key up the nearest pole and tell Plainview about it quick. I can't climb the damn pole."

Standing in the brush well out of sight, Plimpton and Kitts watched the halted train. Two passengers got out and fired six-guns down the tracks. Both robbers were far out of range. A railroad man arrived with a rifle, but he had no target. The outlaws stood and shook hands. Then they headed away through the brush and downhill from the train.

Kitts stopped a half mile down a long, shallow ravine and grinned. "Smell that?"

"Smell what?"

"Wood smoke," Kitts said. "Our man with the horses has

to be damn close by if that's his fire. All we have to do is follow the drifting smoke, and we find our transportation."

"Hope it ain't far," Plimpton said. "This damn gold is heavy."

Kitts turned and eyed his partner a moment. "Just how much you think that gold is worth?"

"Don't know. I've heard these ten-pound bars of gold go for better than three thousand dollars."

Kitts stood there staring at the canvas bag Plimpton carried. "We got eight, maybe ten thousand dollars in them bags. More cash money than I'll earn the rest of my life."

The redhead scowled. "Don't even think about it, Kitts. Dutch would have you by the balls in two hours, and he'd yank them suckers off you, and start poking out your eyes. We do our job, we get our pay, and we don't even think about getting greedy."

Kitts shrugged. "Hell, just a stray thought. Can't always control them sometimes."

"Like when you did that little Mex girl in Texas two years ago who just happened to have a broken neck?"

"Hell, that was an accident. Told you. Long time ago."

Ten minutes later, they came to the end of the ravine and entered a larger one that had a small creek. Kitts dropped to the ground behind some scrub brush and motioned Plimpton down. "Let's check this out before we barge into anything," Kitts said. "I spotted one man at a fire out there but only two horses. Should be three."

Plimpton took a look. They saw a man hunkered over a small fire ring, nudging a coffeepot into the hot coals. The stranger turned and looked at the lower ravine, shrugged and went back to tending his coffee.

"What do you think?" Kitts asked.

"The other horse could be in that brush down there getting a drink."

"Yeah, could be, but is it?"

"Don't know. We go in cautious. Stay spread apart. We got him two to one. If he don't look right, I'll draw fast."

"With him dead, we'd only need two horses," Kitts said.

"We'll see what happens. The other nag might have broken a leg or something. We go in careful and find out."

"Hell, I know," Kitts growled. "I didn't live this long being foolish."

They stood and walked ahead so they were well in sight of the fire and the man.

"Halloo, the fire," Plimpton called.

The man at the fire stood and shaded his eyes. He wasn't wearing a sidearm. He looked their way and waved.

"Hey, over here. I got the horses." He waited until they came closer. "Hi, you don't know me, I'm Jones. You guys have any trouble?"

"Not much," Plimpton said. "Where's the other mount, or are you walking back to Plainview?"

"Not a chance," Jones said. "She's in that brush getting a drink. Took them in one at a time." He paused. "Looks like you brought the goods."

"Sure as hell did," Kitts said. They walked up to the fire, and Jones held out a cup.

"You guys are just in time for coffee. Thought I'd have to drink this pot all by myself."

"Thanks," Plimpton said, taking the tin cup. "So did the boss change his mind? Thought he was going to meet us here."

Jones shrugged. "He's the boss, so he can change his mind if'n he wants. I just do what I'm told."

Plimpton noticed that Jones was dressed like a town man, and his clothes were new. His wide-brimmed straw hat was fresh off a store shelf. Jones's face was soft and pale, and he was built short and thick. Probably strong as a bull. But he didn't look like he was an outdoors man.

"You boys look like you could do with some help packing them sacks," the coffee brewer said.

"Right as rain in August," Plimpton said. "Just to check, we need to know for sure who you are."

Jones poured another cup of coffee and handed it to

Kitts, then grinned. "Yeah, don't blame you for being cautious, knowing what you're carrying. A man by the name of Dutch told me to meet you here with the horses. You had a train ride, got off at marker eighty-seven out of Plainview. That's why I'm here with three horses to meet you and show you the way back to town."

Plimpton nodded. "Sounds like you're the right party to meet. Guess I counted on Dutch being here himself to take the goods."

"Dutch turned up with a bum leg and asked me to come. I do lots of errands for the man. You have any problems at the train?"

"None to mention," Plimpton said. "We got the goods. Two bars of gold, four boxes of greenbacks, and the two registered sacks of mail."

"Show me," Jones said, clearly impressed. "I never seen that much money before in all my days."

Plimpton opened the sack and took out the two bars of gold. The contact man hefted them, put one down, and tested each by cutting into the bar with a boot knife to be sure it wasn't lead dipped in gold.

"Yep, the guaranteed product," he said. "Cash money, too?"

Kitts fished out the four eight-inch-square cardboard boxes that had federal bank notes inside and held them up.

Jones put down the gold, slit open the wrappings on the boxes with his knife, and checked. "Yep, all here and all twenties." He nodded. "Not that I don't trust you boys, but I earn my pay by being careful." He checked the greenbacks in the other boxes in the same way to be sure each one held stacks of fresh bills.

"Yep, you boys did good. How much Dutch say he'd pay you for this little job?"

"Three hundred dollars each," Kitts said. He tossed the mail sacks at the man's feet. "They was two bags of registered, so we brung both. I'd say we earned our pay right well."

Jones sipped his coffee. "Dutch said I should pay you off here. No need for you to come back to town." He grinned at them, threw the rest of his coffee into the fire, and suddenly dropped to the ground.

A second later, a rifle snarled from the brush forty yards away. Plimpton took a heavy round in the chest and staggered backward a step before he slammed to the ground. Kitts had time to reach for his six-gun, but he forgot the cup of coffee in his right hand. It got in the way and spilled down his leg.

The second rifle round hit Kitts in the side of the head. It exploded out the top, taking six inches of his skull with it. Kitts jolted to the side, a sudden corpse, and sprawled in the Missouri dirt.

Jones, who had gone flat in the dust near the fire, stood and waved at the brush. He took a derringer from his pocket and watched Plimpton. He saw the robber struggle to lift one hand. Jones grunted and fired a round into Plimpton's head. The train robber gave one last spasm before his head rolled to the side.

Forty yards upstream, a man stepped out of the brush with a rifle in his hand. He trotted to the fire and looked at the two dead men.

"You're sure the goods are all there?" the rifleman asked. He wore a town hat, fancy pants, and a silk shirt. He had a hawk face and was no more than twenty-five years old.

"Oh, yeah, Brady, it's all there. I made sure of that. Let's get back to town. All this outdoor work is driving me crazy."

3

Fargo and Betty had just started breakfast at the Farm House Café when a clerk from the railroad office rushed up.

"Mr. Fargo, they need you over at the office right now. Train got robbed and the Express car blown up about a half hour ago."

Fargo stood at once, put two silver dollars on the table, and touched Betty's shoulder. "You have breakfast. I won't see you for a while. I have some work to do."

He trotted to the railroad station and into the district manager's office. There were ten people there waiting for him.

Neville looked up, patted his balding head with a linen handkerchief. "Fargo, about time you got here. This is what came over the wire twenty-five minutes ago." He handed Fargo a yellow paper with hand printing.

ENGINE 460 WESTBOUND OUT OF ST. LOUIS ROBBED BY TWO ARMED MEN NEAR THE EIGHTY-SEVENTH MARKER AT 9:40 A.M. TODAY. EXPRESS CAR BLOWN OPEN, SAFE BLASTED AND EMPTIED. EXPRESS MAN KILLED, CONDUCTOR WOUNDED. TRAIN CONTINUING WESTWARD AT 9:54. NOW DUE IN PLAINVIEW, ESTIMATED 10:42 A.M.

Fargo dropped the paper and frowned. "How far is mile marker eighty-seven from here?"

"It's about twenty-six miles to the east," someone said.

"How soon do you have an eastbound train? Repair, work, freight, anything?"

Neville looked at the dispatcher. "Wilbur?"

"We have a switch engine and two work cars leaving here eastbound as soon as the string that was robbed gets here. Looks to be about ten forty-five. Depending on old Engine Four-Sixty."

"Hook up a cattle car so I can load on my horse. I'll need cleat boards for getting out. Let me off at mile marker eighty-seven. First I'll want to talk to the wounded conductor." Fargo looked at the new pocket watch he had bought. Since he was going to be in town for a while, he had figured he might need one. Townies tended to use the clock a lot. "That leaves me twenty-eight minutes to saddle my Ovaro and get on board." He turned to leave.

"Mr. Fargo," Neville said. "These filthy robbers killed one of our own and wounded a conductor. I want those killers. Make sure you bring them in dead or alive."

Fargo nodded and hurried out of the office.

At the livery stable he found the Ovaro in the small pasture behind the stable. He whistled, and the black and white pinto pricked up his ears, turned, and trotted over to the gate. Fargo rubbed the big animal's ears and patted his neck. The pinto's fore- and hindquarters were jet black and the midsection creamy white.

It took Fargo five minutes to comb down the pinto and saddle him. His saddlebags carried a supply of beef jerky. He filled a two-quart flat canteen and tied it on, then rode the Ovaro down the street to the depot and up on the freight platform. After tying the Ovaro to a luggage cart, Fargo sat down and waited.

Fifteen minutes later, a train came rolling in. The engine number was 460. Two dozen train men and townsmen, including the doctor, were there. They took the conductor off first and put him in a wheelchair. Neville talked to him, then Fargo had his turn.

"Can you describe the killers?"

"Oh, yes. Never forget them. One was tall, young, and redheaded. Said his name was Plimpton. Second man was a head shorter and had a paunch. Wore a brown cowboy hat and tied-down six-gun."

"That's enough," Dr. Andrews said. "I need this man in my office to tend to his leg." He waved, and a man pushed the chair away toward the town side of the tracks. Fargo went back to where he had left the pinto on the freight platform.

As soon as the 460 train headed west, a work string came on the main line and pulled up to the platform with an added boxcar with the big door open. The pinto had no problem going into the dark hole of the boxcar. He'd been on many like it before. Fargo dismounted, tied the reins to a bar on the side of the car, and welcomed the bale of hay that a freight handler rolled up on a hand truck. Fargo sat on the hay, leaned against the far side of the boxcar, and had a perfect window on this part of Missouri out the open door for the next twenty-six miles.

Fargo figured the robbers must have jumped off the train while it was still moving. Otherwise, the passengers and trainmen would have seen them. It wouldn't be hard to find where two men had jumped and rolled off a rail car. They must have carried or thrown off their loot in heavy bags or maybe even mail sacks. Fargo decided to start his search a quarter mile before the mile marker and continue for a half mile past it.

At a steady thirty-five miles an hour the work engine jolted the short train to the east. They would hit the eighty-seven-mile marker in about forty-five minutes. Skye watched the fertile countryside flash by. Lots of farms and small towns were starting to emerge. In a hundred years this would be solid farms and towns and maybe even cities. It would be interesting to come back in a century and look at all the changes, Fargo mused.

He spotted three barefoot boys fishing with long poles at the edge of a good-size stream, then later saw a half dozen boys diving into a river. Missouri didn't lack for trees. The state had a wide range of hardwoods, from oak to ash and hickory and even some bald cypress in the wetter areas.

Fargo closed his eyes and took a short nap. The train whistle woke him, and he looked outside and saw mile marker eighty-eight flash past. He got the cleat planks ready to reach the four-foot drop to the ground. He could jump the Ovaro out, but he wasn't sure what kind of footing there would be beside the tracks.

The train began slowing a few minutes later, and Fargo saw the next mile marker come up. The train coasted a hundred yards shy of the marker, where there was a nearly level spot. The brakeman directed the engineer to the exact spot and the train stopped. Fargo put down the four cleated planks to give the Ovaro room to walk on. Then he was off the train and gone, riding three hundred yards back along the way they had come. He heard the train start up and pull away, heading on eastward. Fargo moved onto the side of the right-of-way, walking the pinto, checking and evaluating every clump of bushes and grass that grew on the right-hand bank. The train tracks burrowed their way through a solid stand of cottonwood and maples with a few elms in the fringes.

The country here was similar to most of the northern half of Missouri: gentle hills, open fertile plains, and well-watered prairies. This stretch included one of the rolling hills and a sharp gully to the left. The train was on an upward slope here and probably was not at full speed during the robbery, Fargo decided.

This was the country of the coneflower and larkspur, of deer and elk, bear and still some bison here and there, with otter and beaver in the rivers.

He was truly in his element. He knew about the plains and the woods. He could interpret the signs on the land, of the bushes, the wind, and the very earth itself. He had developed a special sensitivity to the land and its animals and plants. It kept him alive, it enabled him to track and trail men and animals that few men in the nation could. Fargo had learned to be a part of all nature, yet he was still able to draw back from it and interpret it and use it, much as the Indian had learned to do over the centuries. He could live as one with nature, but not be limited to it.

Fargo picked out a deer trail that crossed the tracks and vanished into the heavy growth of mixed cottonwood and maple. To one side he found the skeleton of a deer that might have been hit by a fast-moving train. Nothing else disturbed the natural growth along the tracks. He rode slowly, covering each square foot of ground twice.

At the eighty-seven-mile marker he paused and let his gaze take in the long view up and down the side of the tracks. He wasn't sure he was even on the right side of the rails. The express cars had doors that opened on both sides, depending on the station's platform. The robbers could have jumped either way.

Maybe. The mile markers were on this side. The robbers would have watched for the marker and probably opened the door on the left as the train moved up the grade. He viewed the scene ahead of him with long sweeping gazes, and stared hard at an area about thirty yards down the tracks. He spotted marks in the grass, weeds, and small bushes, and rode quickly to the spot, still checking the area from the marker to the damaged area.

As he came closer, Fargo could see definite marks showing where something had disturbed the natural growth of the grass and weeds. One small bush had been bent over and broken off, as if a man had crashed down the slope. He dismounted and studied the area again. A one-eyed man in a thunderstorm could find this spot. The heavy tracks of two men moved into the elm and sweet gum twenty yards from the tracks. From the sign it looked like the men had lain there for some time, then moved on downhill.

Fargo whistled for the Ovaro, which pranced down the right-of-way on easy footing, then down the bank where Fargo waited. He slapped the animal on the neck and rubbed his ears, then mounted. Skye could follow this blind man's trail from the saddle.

The track led downgrade for a half mile, working past more stands of cottonwood and maple, then followed a gully that emptied into a small valley with a stream in it. He saw where the men had hunkered down behind some bushes. They had set down four heavy bags. All had made plain impressions in the soft ground.

A new smell tingled Fargo's nostrils. A foreign scent that had nothing to do with the surrounding natural elements. A wisp of smoke from an almost dead campfire. He turned and sniffed again. The scent came from upstream. He studied the ground. The two men's footprints went across some loose sand and up along the bank of the stream.

Suddenly the tracks were gone. Fargo rode back ten feet and read the trail again. He hadn't seen them turn to the left into the stream. The pinto waded across the water that was only two feet deep at the center. The tracks showed on the far side and continued upstream.

Fargo caught another whiff of the campfire. He looked ahead and saw the blackened scar of charcoal on the brown sand of the streambank. The tracks led directly toward it.

Fargo worked forward, then circled the campfire, studying the sign left there. He figured there were four men. Two with cowboy boot heels, another one with a slightly wider heel, and a fourth with town shoes, broad sole and heel. Four men, two met by two. The pungent smell of coffee filtered through the noontime air. He could see where splashes of the liquid had put out most of the fire.

He identified two different sets of hoofprints. Both were

20

shod, and both had been in place for some time, with droppings sprinkling where they probably were ground-tied.

In one spot the cowboy boots seemed to be facing the
tracks of the town-shoe man. The marks were three feet
apart, aimed exactly at the other one. Just behind the boot
prints, Fargo saw the heavy and wide mark of what could
be a man's body stretched in the dirt. He found a dark
reddish-brown spot he was sure was blood. Another blood
stain showed almost two feet above that. Nearby he saw
what had to be a part of a human skull with hair still attached.

Near the fire, Fargo found another place where a body
could have dropped into the dirt. There was no blood here.
A plain trail gouged into the dirt showed where both bodies
had been dragged into the edge of the hickory and short-
leaf pine trees twenty feet from the campfire.

Fargo stopped at the edge of the trees. With signs pointing to two dead bodies, and no circling buzzards or hawks,
Fargo knew there were two shallow graves nearby. There
was no sign of the mail sacks or any Railway Express
items.

One body had been dragged through a six-foot-wide car-
pet of goldenrod and wild asters. The trail led under the
short-leaf pines and up a slight slope about thirty feet under
the trees when it ended. Someone had tried to conceal the
grave by throwing branches and some grass and forest
mulch on top of the newly turned earth.

He went back to the campfire and found the other drag
trail, which led along the stream bank for fifty feet before it
turned sharply into the pines and ending at a second grave
ten feet inside the tree line. Fargo dropped to his knees at
the edge of the dug-up earth. He had to know. He found a
broken-off branch and used it to loosen the soil. Then he
scooped it out with his hands. He worked one end, hoping
it was the right one.

A foot down, he unearthed a hand. He worked more
carefully as he dug around it. Then another six inches down

he came to the head. He removed just enough of the dirt and leaves to get a firm description of the body, then covered it up again.

At the second grave, Fargo hit the wrong end and came up with cowboy boots. He went to the other end of the grave and soon had the second man's head exposed. This one was more distinctive, with lots of red hair and fair skin. He also had a scar on his left cheek.

The Trailsman covered the second body, memorized the spot where he was, and whistled for the Ovaro. It trotted up to Fargo and stood in front of him. Fargo mounted the pinto and rode back to trace the horseshoe prints. There seemed to be a mishmash of tracks, and he had to circle the fire at fifty feet to nail down the double set of prints that headed west toward Plainview. Fargo wondered if the two killers would go all the way through the trees and brush, or would they branch off toward the old stage road and head east away from the town?

Ten minutes later, Fargo had one question answered. He came across a litter of paper under the trees. He dismounted and checked it and knew it was the registered mail. They had even left the two heavy burlap postal bags. Fargo stared at the trashed mail for a full minute, then bent down and began to pick up the papers and letters and stuff them into one of the burlap bags.

It took him two hours to gather up all of the pieces of paper and envelopes and torn-up letters on the forest floor. The torn-up mail was scattered out more than a hundred feet, and he did most of it on his hands and knees. The torn-up paper took more room than the original mail had, and Fargo had to cram the last pieces into the sacks to get everything inside. He tied the bags together, circled the ropes around his chest, and let the bags hang down his back. Better than spooking the Ovaro with the clumsy things banging on his hindquarters for twenty-four more miles.

An hour later, he was still tracking the pair of mounts,

heading up a long valley to the west that would come out near the railroad and the stage road beyond it.

The trail had wound higher, and Fargo checked the sun through the canopy of sweet gum and elm. He figured it should be a little after three in the afternoon. Then he remembered his pocket watch and pulled it out on its rawhide leash and opened the front. The watch showed 3:10. What did he need a watch for? He brayed a laugh and grinned.

Another hour of easy tracking and he came to the railroad. The pair of riders had paused there and let their mounts eat some of the new grass. Then they had crossed the tracks and headed due north for the old stage road. When the riders had paused beside the road, one of the horses relieved itself. Skye stepped down from his mount and felt the horse biscuits. They were no longer warm. In this weather they would cool down in about four hours. He had to be at least five, maybe six hours behind the pair. No chance he could catch them before they hit Plainview—if they were going there, and if they didn't stop for the night somewhere. If they had camped, he would have a chance to catch them.

Fargo kneed the Ovaro into a canter. He could cover six miles in an hour this way. A walking horse covered four. It was easy riding on the old stagecoach road. A few small trees had taken root and lots of grass and shrubs had sprung up, but there were few washouts and no fallen-down bridges. A little after five-thirty he pulled up the pinto to a walk.

Fargo dug out some beef jerky and chewed on a slab. The dried beef would provide him with enough energy to keep him going for several days. He had another two hours of light before he'd have to decide what to do. He would ride into the night, or stop for some sleep and head on in tomorrow.

At seven-thirty, he decided he had about ten more miles to town. He'd ride on. He moved the mail bags to a pack in back of his saddle and rode on. With any luck he should hit town just about ten o'clock. The café would still be open, which would be a welcome change from the jerky.

It was 9:50 when Fargo rode up to the post office and swung down the two Railway Express bags. Two men came out of the shadows and pounced on the bags. One held up a silver badge Fargo had never seen before.

"Larson, U.S. postal inspector. We were almost here when we heard about the robbery. Those the bags?"

"Right. The mail is ripped up and tattered, but I found every shred. Gonna be a patchwork puzzle."

"That's my job. I have help and a room with big tables. We'll be working around the clock until we put it back together. We have the register logs from the last clerk. We'll check it off and see if anything is missing."

"It's all yours." Fargo turned and led the pinto to the Farm Home Café. He wanted a huge steak, three baked potatoes, a bucket of gravy, and all the coffee he could guzzle. He took his time eating, savoring every bite. After he paid the check, he put the Ovaro in the stable and had it wiped down and fed.

As Fargo came out of the livery, two men watched him from the shadows in front of a saloon across the street.

"So he found the mail sacks. We figured somebody would. Don't hurt us a bit." The larger of the two men spoke softly. He wore an expensive suit, and a gold chain linked his vest pockets. In the center of the chain hung a gold nugget the size of a marble.

"Somebody had to go look for it," the second man said. "That's about all the good it's going to do them." He was rail thin and wore a brown suit and black bowler. He touched snuff to his nose and summarily sneezed. "That is absolutely all that mister railroad detective is going to learn," the thin man said with a touch of authority. "If he wants to stay healthy, that better be all he digs up about this little matter of the train robbery."

4

Earlier that same evening Jones and Brady had ridden toward a small house near the north edge of Plainview. They had paused in a copse of flowering hawthorne trees fifty yards from the frame building. One lamp burned in the front window, but no other lights showed in the house. Brady nodded.

"Looks right to me. No horses in front or back. One light. Just the way the man said it would be."

The smaller man, Jones, hesitated. He was older, had lived longer by being cautious, as he often told his younger partner. He scratched his stubbled chin.

"You go up to the door and check it out. I'll stay here with the goods. If it ain't right, you start shooting. If they double-cross us, we'll hightail it out of here with the gold and the cash, understand?"

Brady grinned in the darkness. "Oh, yeah, I know. Fact is, I kind of hope they try something along them lines, just so we can blast them into hell and keep the goods."

"Don't hope for it. If trouble starts, you'll be the first one they gut-shoot straight into hell. Get up there and try the door. Knock like you are an honest man."

Brady nodded, his face a bit grimmer now, and rode to the house. He dismounted, let the reins ground-tie his mount, then walked to the door and knocked.

The door swung inward, and a man's figure appeared, bathed in the light from inside. The two talked a moment, then Brady waved, and Jones, still mounted, rode up and dismounted.

He walked to the door. "Is this the right house for a pair of strangers in town?" Jones asked.

The man inside, Phil Ingram, grinned. "Cautious, I like that. I'll tell the boss. You got the goods?" The speaker stood five-four, wore a six-gun on his left hip, and although he said he was twenty-eight years old, he was totally bald.

"We get what we go after," Jones said. He was built broad and low to the ground with heavily muscled shoulders that spoke of long hours spent in a mine. He wore town clothes and shoes, but his tanned and weathered face revealed his rural roots. He pushed back his hat and frowned. "Still not sure this is the right place. How much are we getting paid for this job?"

"Cautious to the end," Ingram said. "You both get five hundred in cash as soon as you deliver, and after I confirm that the goods are present and intact." Ingram stared hard at Jones. "What are you supposed to do as soon as you get paid?"

"Easy," Brady said. "We catch the first train out of town going east, and we don't spend more than ten dollars apiece in town before we go."

"Good, you have it right," Ingram said. "Bring in the goods, I'll check them over, and then you two will get paid and be on your way."

Brady looked at his companion, who nodded. Brady hurried out the door and a few moments later came back with the heavy canvas bags that held the two bars of gold, the four boxes of bank notes, and six registered mail envelopes that had been ripped open.

Brady swung the bags onto a cheap table and backed away. Ingram looked at the gold bars, saw where they had been knife-checked before, and nodded. Then he opened one box of greenbacks and saw that none of the bands had been broken. His face remained serious as he checked the other boxes of bank notes, then the registered envelopes.

Two of them held jewelry, one a set of legal papers, another had an old book in it, and the others contained more official-looking papers and certificates.

"The pretty goods are here. I don't know about the legal documents and the other stuff. Not my job." He reached inside one of the boxes of twenties, broke a bank band, and counted out a thousand dollars. He gave each man five hundred.

"I know you're both professionals, but don't go off half cocked and miss that eastbound train. It leaves the depot at six thirty-two a.m. Be sure you're on it. As an added incentive, if you're not on that train, some vicious men will hunt you down and kill you on the spot. Remember, don't spend more than ten dollars before you get on the train."

The two killers grinned at the cash. "Holy damn," Brady whispered. "Ain't never seen this much cash money in my whole life."

"Just the start of our partnership, kid," Jones said. "Let's get out of here and find a big supper somewhere and then a soft bed. Hey, in a few days we'll be in St. Louis, with more girls, whiskey, and food than you can imagine."

Ingram stepped back and picked up a sawed-off shotgun. He held it so it wasn't pointing directly at the two riders, but not far off.

"Just a small precaution, gentlemen. Now, if you'll walk out of here slowly and make no sudden moves, we won't have any accidents. We don't want any problems, do we?"

Jones chuckled. "Hey, you won't get any trouble from us. We know our place. I couldn't figure out what to do with the kind of money that's on the table anyway." He shook his head. "Come on, kid, let's get out of here."

Brady and Jones backed their way slowly to the door, went out, and closed it behind them. Ingram darted to the side of the room, where he could see out the window. He watched through the darkness until he saw both men riding away into the night. Only then did he let out a long sigh and lower the shotgun.

"It's all right to come out now. Both of them are gone and the goods are all here."

Two men came through the second door in the small living room. One was six-two, heavily built and wore a suit that cost him fifty dollars in St. Louis, five times what most men paid for their suits. A gold chain connected the vest pockets. In the center of the chain hung a gold nugget the size of a shooting marble.

The second man wore a brown suit of much lesser quality and a black bowler. He was so thin he looked sickly. Just as they came into the room, he touched snuff to his nose and sneezed. The men hurried to the table and checked the gold, then the bank notes. The large man nodded, waving at the papers. "Too much reading material for now, Dutch," he said. "We'll look them over at the office."

Dutch stepped over to the bald man, who had stood watching them. "What did we say we'd pay you, Baldy?"

"Please, my name is Ingram, Phil Ingram. You said it was worth two hundred dollars to meet them, collect the goods, and pay them off."

Dutch frowned and turned back toward his partner. "Did we say two hundred for Baldy here?" When he turned back he had a six-inch knife in his hand, and before Ingram could shout or move, the blade swung out and slashed deeply across his throat. It sliced open the left carotid artery, and blood spurted out.

Ingram screamed and staggered sideways. His hands came up to cover the pulsating spurts of blood but couldn't contain them. Each time his heart beat, the blood pressure geysered a gout of blood six feet across the room. He turned and looked at the two men with surprise and terror. Ingram tried to draw his six-gun with his blood-slippery left hand, but it slid off the butt. Dutch knocked Ingram's hand away, pulled out Ingram's pistol, and pushed him to the floor. He fell hitting hard on his side. Blood still spurted from his carotid as he rolled onto his back.

"Why?" Ingram choked out. "What did I do wrong?"

"Nothing wrong, Baldy," Dutch said. "We break the chain, cover our tracks. Nobody can ever trace the robbery back to us with no witnesses. Nothing personal, just the way we do business."

The heavy man glanced only once at Ingram, then pushed everything back into the bags and carried them to the door.

"Finish up here and I'll see you at the office. We have a lot of work to do tonight."

Kirk Gaylord stood at the small Plainview U.S. Post Office counter. It was nine o'clock the morning after the train robbery, and the postmistress had told him once before that she hadn't received any registered mail for him.

"Sorry, Mr. Gaylord, still nothing at all came for you," Mrs. Olson said. In her fifties, she pushed gray hair back from her face with one hand. Then she fussed with a broach on her dress. "You know about the train robbery. I hear that two sacks of registered matter were stolen. Lord knows, it'll be days before we see any of it. You said you had a small parcel that was due?"

"Yes, Mrs. Olson. Some extremely important documents from St. Louis. What happens if the robbers kept some of the registered mail?"

"Usually they stop somewhere and open everything, looking for money and jewelry, stocks and bonds. Now and then the U.S. Treasury sends cash through the registered mail."

Gaylord nodded and twice almost broke in, but waited until she finished. He was a tall, robust man with neatly cut blond hair, no mustache or face whiskers, and soft blue eyes.

"So what happens to the stolen mail?"

"Oh, they already found it. Railroad sent a detective out to look for it and the robbers. The man brought the torn-up registered matter in late last night."

"Then that's the registered mail that scattered all over those tables down at the railroad station?"

"No room here to sort it out." She stopped and a frown touched her face. "I know what you're missing must be mighty important to you. I do hope you get it back."

Gaylord touched the brim of his brown fedora. "Indeed I do, too." He turned and looked back. "Would they mind if I stopped by at the station and asked about my registered mail?"

"Can't hurt, but won't do no good. Registered matter is like sacred with the post office. By now they have a postal inspector here from St. Louis checking every envelope and torn-up piece of paper."

"Damn," Gaylord said. His expression changed into an angry frown. For a moment his furious expression frightened Mrs. Olson. She took a half step back from the counter and squinted at him.

Gaylord cleared his throat and looked away, then lifted his brows. His dark expression vanished. "Sorry, Mrs. Olson. This isn't your fault. Thanks for your time." He walked out of the store, leaving the postmistress with a small frown on her round face.

Kirk Gaylord walked the block and a half to the train station. He became more worried and upset as he marched along. The family lawyer in St. Louis had assured him that the package would be as safe as if it were in his very own hands.

It should have arrived yesterday, ready for pickup. The damn train robbery. At once he had suspected foul play. His brother and sister would both love to see the package destroyed and never brought to light in a court of law. Yes, they would gain a lot if the package was lost or torn to pieces. He had told them they were being treated in the will the same way they had treated their father in his last troubled years. They had ignored their ill father, squandered his money, hadn't visited him. Didn't deserve to be in the will at all.

He entered the station and walked up to the ticket counter. The stationmaster recognized him and came to meet him.

"What can I do for you today, Mr. Gaylord?"

Gaylord hesitated. Perhaps he was being too public about all of this. Anyone watching him would surely be able to see that he was distraught, on the edge of fury and worried well past simple frustration. Yet he plunged on.

"The registered mail. Are they done sorting it so I can sign for mine and pick it up?"

"Afraid not. Bound to be another day, maybe even two, before they get it all put back together. First they have to check each of the recorded registration numbers to be sure it's all there."

"Some might be missing?"

"That's why men steal the bags, looking for jewelry, cash, gold, anything of value."

"Couldn't I just take a look?"

"That I can answer. Nobody, not even me, can even look in that room until they have all the answers. Way he's storming around, it's my guess there was a lot of money missing from that shipment. Could be some criminal charges and maybe prosecutions here. The trainmen would be responsible, and could face prison."

A dark look swept over Gaylord's face again as he turned and stormed away. He clenched his fists at his sides, and he knew his face was turning red. How could this be happening? The lawyer had assured him there would be no trouble. There was one legal copy of the will and that was it. It had been inconvenient for Gaylord to go to St. Louis and pick up the documents. Neither could the lawyer take the time to hand-carry them to Plainview. After all, everyone trusted the U.S. registered mail. Now Gaylord knew that he could trust no one, not even his lawyer.

The next morning, Fargo awoke promptly at five. Last night he had slipped into bed quietly, not awaking Betty.

Now he looked up to see her spread out over him, gently kissing him awake.

"Hey, there, I missed you last night."

"Dead tired."

"Too tired?"

"Then, not now." He returned her kisses, then rolled her over gently and stripped the sheet from between them. She slept naked, and he stared down at her. A flowing surf of pure black hair framing her smiling face with the high cheekbones, and a thin aquiline nose slightly tipped up, and darting, luminous green eyes. Her round face had a smile to match the sunrise.

"We have plenty of time before you need to go back to the old railroad, right?" She reached up and traced a finger along his chin, up to his forehead and back down, then leaned up and kissed his lips, exploring his open mouth with her tongue.

She sighed and lay back on the bed. He lifted her to a sitting position, and watched her big breasts bounce and sway. Delicious. They had large pink areolas and darker pink nipples that were starting to surge upward with hot passion. She had a generous waist and wide hips that tapered down to strong legs.

He bent and kissed her breasts, and she sucked in a breath and moaned softly, her hands working into the dark hair on the back of his head and holding his face to her bosom.

Fargo kissed the delicious orbs, then licked the nipples, watching them grow to nearly thumb size. Then he sucked one tasty breast into his mouth and chewed gently on the softly yielding flesh.

"Oh, yes, darling, yes, yes. I love it when you do that. Now the other one so she won't get jealous. Tits are serious about equal treatment." He moved his mouth and went through the ritual again, biting her nipple first until she yelped softly.

"Oh, Fargo, bite me again, again, again." Her moans increased with his fervent nibbling, and then she gave a huge sigh and tilted backward, pulling him on top of her.

While he worked on her breasts, she had been busy with her hands. She found his stiffening rod between his legs and gently stroked it, then simply held him with one hand, feeling his engorged tool throbbing with excitement.

Fargo lifted away from her breasts and trailed kisses down her chest, over her ribs, and across her soft belly, where he tongued out her belly button, then moved farther south.

"Oh, God, yes, Fargo, sweetness. Down there, yes, down there." Her moans came often, and he felt her hips writhing under him. He lifted his mouth and moved both hands to her feet. Fargo massaged them vigorously, then began working both hands up her ankles and to her calves, and then just past her knee.

"Hurry, darling, Oh, please hurry. You know where it is. Find it, lover. Find it soon."

Her hips gyrated wildly on the thin sheet. The bed began to squeak, but she didn't hear it. Fargo's talented fingers caressed up her inner thighs, stroked them around and up and down, and caused her to thrash her hips more. His fingers trailed around her soft black bush at her crotch, and she let out a wail of disappointment.

"You lost down there, lover? Don't know where you're going?"

He chuckled and trailed back down and touched her moist nest, then parted the pink lips and massaged them as she writhed under his touch. He leaned up and kissed her, driving his tongue into her mouth, exploring. At the same time he thrust one finger deep into her honeyed cavity, bringing a whoop of delight.

The kiss lasted for a dozen strokes with his finger. Then he found the tiny bud of her clit, and he strummed it three, four, then five times. Betty let out a gasp. Her hips pounded straight up at him as spasm after spasm shook her body, and she whimpered and cried, and then let out a long keening scream that Fargo figured they could hear all the way to the hundred-mile marker.

Betty gave one final hump with her hips, and settled down and looked up at him. "Nobody ever done me so damn good that way before," she said. "Now I'm really wound up for the main course. Think you can stomach it?"

Fargo went over her, spread her pure white legs, and drove forward in one smooth move. Betty yelped and then moaned in delight as he penetrated and thrust inward until their pelvic bones ground together.

"Yes, lover man, yes. Do me. Do me good. Oh, God, yes!"

Then Fargo was on his own roller coaster and knew he couldn't stop. He pounded harder and felt her climax again, soaring into the sky with her soft wail and her counter thrusts at his hips. Fargo felt the whole universe coming apart as his passion built and built. Then it did explode, and he was jetted over the moon and into a star field before he came smashing back down, giving one last furious thrust with his hips. He dropped his whole weight on her as he felt his spring-tight body begin to slacken and loosen, and then a long sigh escaped.

Betty's arms circled his back. She was still panting from her fourth climax, and she came down slowly. She whispered to him all the while. He heard little of it, still too keyed up to understand the words.

"Yes, lover, Skye. What a glorious way to start the day. Promise me we can start every day this way."

He mumbled something, his breath still coming in short gasps as he recovered.

"Love you pushing down hard on me this way, sinking me into the mattress. God, but I'm hungry. Let's get dressed and go have about a hundred flapjacks and good maple syrup and a whole plate full of bacon and a gallon of coffee."

Fargo lifted off her and sat on the edge of the bed. He grinned and nodded at the idea of breakfast. He could use some food to get his strength back. It was going to be a tough day with the damn railroad boss yelling at him.

Just before eight o'clock, Fargo walked into the district manager's office, after he had checked on the Ovaro. It had plenty of water, and Fargo told the stable hand to give him another ration of oats.

Neville looked up and scowled. "St. Louis is furious with everyone within fifty miles of this robbery and murder. The big payoff might have been by chance. There were two gold bars and over twenty thousand dollars in fresh greenbacks in that safe." Neville grabbed a cigar from the humidor on his desk, bit off the end and lit it, then blew a mouthful of smoke at the ceiling. He scratched his chin, and his face was wreathed with anger and worry.

"You said you didn't find a damn thing up there in the hills to help us. No broken horseshoe print, or a dropped hat, or anything?"

"No. Two riders evidently shot the two men who pulled the train robbery. They must have been professionals and knew exactly what to do and how to hide it. They figured the bodies wouldn't be found."

"So right now we have nothing. No descriptions. We think they brought the goods right here to town. Is that right?"

"About the size of it. I'm going to talk to the conductor and the brakeman. They might have remembered something. The two robbers evidently bought tickets somewhere. I'm on it."

Ten minutes later, he found Wendell Mannington sitting in the freight office at the depot. "Figured you'd be home in bed taking it easy," Fargo said.

Mannington shrugged, and the movement hurt his leg. He winced. "Tried that. All the excitement is down here. Tried to get into the place where they're sorting the mail garbage you brought back, but they booted my ass out of there."

"How's the leg?"

"Hurts like hell. You've been shot, you know the feeling. I try not to think about it when I'm down here." He gingerly moved the leg, and pain fluttered across his face. "You want to talk about the robbery, I guess. I jawed with the postal guys. Idiots, all of them. Not at all concerned with the cash and gold we lost from the safe."

"Not their problem. If I described two men to you, could you tell me if they're the ones who robbed the train?"

"Damn right. You caught them already?"

"In a way. Was one of them in his twenties, tall and red-headed?"

"Yeah. You must have caught the bastard to know that. That damned red hair. He's the one who told me his name and to remember it, because he robbed trains. I owe that one a punch in the nose. He's the one who shot me."

"What about the other one? Was he older, maybe in his forties, had a knife scar on one cheek?"

"My God, come to think on it, the shorter one did have a scar. Didn't think much about it at the time. I was busy trying to stay alive. Yeah, a scar and black hair. You caught the bastards."

"Yeah, and they can't rob any more trains. Both of them are in shallow graves in the hills about a mile from where the train stopped after the robbery."

"Damn good! You kill them?"

"Nope. Dead and buried when I found them. Two men on horseback met them. My guess is they shot the robbers, buried them, and then rode here to Plainview."

"Don't say? So maybe the killers are here in town right now?"

"Could be, but my bet is that they took the first train out of town heading east. Mr. Mannington, do you remember hearing the robbers say anything about who they were meeting, or who hired them?"

The conductor thought a moment, then shook his head. He moved his wounded leg so it rested on a chair. "Damn, no. Didn't use names, I listened for that especially. I been

36

robbed before. They were tight-lipped, knew what they were doing. That redhead shot me, then they blew the Express car door, killed Jenkins, and looted the car and the safe. When the train slowed down, they went out the side door of the Express car."

"What about the Express man? You know him?"

"Just to say howdy. He rode my trains a few times. He lived in St. Louis. The agent is responsible for the mail and what's in the safe. They check it and sign it over from one man to the next."

"Any way he could have been connected to the robbery? Perhaps he left the safe open or something. Maybe he told someone there was lots of cash and gold in the safe."

"Not a chance, not Jenkins. If he helped them, why would they kill him?"

"To cover their trail. It's happened before, the double-cross." Fargo turned to the door. "I better check with the post office guys. Maybe they've found something. At least we know now that the two dead men were the robbers. Take care of that leg."

At the other end of the depot, Fargo found the room where the mail was being pieced back together. He knocked, and the same inspector he'd seen the night before opened the door and stepped outside.

"Well, well, the detective. Looks like you found almost all of the mail. We've checked the numbers and have all of them except for six. The Treasury Department wired us the numbers on those twenty-dollar bills. I gave them to the sheriff. He wasn't happy about giving the numbers to the local merchants. Said few folks in this town ever saw twenty dollars in cash at one time."

"I'll talk to the sheriff about it. You say you found all the registered mail except six pieces. Where are they?"

"Maybe destroyed or stolen. Did the robbers build a fire where they tore up the mail?"

"No fire."

"So we have to contact those six people who sent the

registered mail and find out what it was and how much it was worth. We'll have to pay for the value."

"Could the robbers have been hunting for a specific item in the registered sacks?"

"Could have. Or maybe they took the mail as an afterthought, knowing they had scored big with the gold and cash."

"Which doesn't help us find whoever is behind the robbery."

"You want those serial numbers?"

Fargo said he did. The inspector took out a pad from his pocket and wrote down the numbers.

"Go from A67034000 to A67034999. That's a thousand bills in the twenty denomination. Hope this helps. Could be a week before we can identify the people whose parcels we can't find. One even lives in New York City. I have a man sending telegrams to them right now."

"When will the mail get back in motion?"

"Local registered will be done this afternoon. Rest will go back into a registered sack heading on west to the end of this line."

Outside the station, Fargo headed for the temporary courthouse and the small sheriff's office in one corner. Matt Crosby was the sheriff's name. Fargo had never met him. The courthouse was a former two-story dry goods store that had gone out of business five years ago. The county bought it as a temporary courthouse.

The sheriff was in. Crosby was a thick-set man with an expanded waistline and carrying fifty too many pounds. His face was round and stubbled, he had black hair, was soft-looking, and had bags under sharp eyes that missed nothing.

"Yeah, you're that Trailsman the rail boys brought in. You found the two bodies. We need to go out and bury them again?"

"Not my suggestion. I can give you descriptions. One of

them called himself Red Plimpton, according to the wounded conductor."

"Give me a report of fifty words about what you found, the names and descriptions of those involved, and I'll file it. No sense going back out there to rebury those two killers."

Fargo took a pencil and paper and wrote out the information and handed it to the sheriff. "Anything turn up on those twenty-dollar bills yet?"

"Not yet and not likely. I told two barkeeps about it and they hooted at me. They said they hadn't seen a twenty-dollar bill for a month."

"It's still the right thing to do. If you didn't talk to the bank, I'll go over there."

The sheriff waved at him and went back to looking over wanted posters. Fargo headed for the First Plains Bank. This was not the part of his work that Fargo enjoyed, but it had to be done. Digging out the facts, laying them straight, trying to track the case step by step. Most train robberies had cause and effects to find and follow. So far he didn't even have the first clue what had happened.

The banker, Vernon Zilke, nodded curtly when Fargo told him about the missing bills.

"Heard about it. Twenty thousand laying around somewhere. Damn shame it got stolen."

"Hoping some of it will be spent here in town. I can give you the serial numbers to watch for."

"Right, be glad to. We don't handle more than half a dozen twenties all day, so it won't be a trouble. Most of the big bills come from the stores or the saloons. Most saloons don't have an account here. I always wondered about that. I mean, with the drinking and drunkenness, and sometimes gunplay, I wouldn't think they'd hide their spare cash on the premises."

The banker took down the serial numbers, and Fargo moved on to the best saloon in town. He asked the barkeep to watch for twenty-dollar bills.

"Got me too much to do to look at the dumb little numbers on any folding money," the first apron said.

At the third saloon, there was a flicker of interest. The place was only a small step up from a barrel bar, with sawdust on the floor and two girls who appraised Fargo from the narrow stairs that led up to a pair of cribs on the second floor.

The barkeep used the name Chic Calhoon. He eyed the serial numbers and nodded.

"They be brand-new bills?"

"Right, uncirculated, bright and shiny. Probably would be used by a stranger in town."

Calhoon let a small frown edge onto his face. "If'n I did take in one of these bills, would it stay mine? I wouldn't know if'n it was stolen or not. Right?"

"Technically, the bills are stolen and can be confiscated by the sheriff."

"But you wouldn't do that?"

"Not if you tell me about the man who passed the bills."

"Let me take a look." Calhoon reached under the bar and came up with a metal cash box with a solid lid. He opened it and on top were three twenty-dollar bills. All were crisp and new. He laid them out side by side on the bar and read off the numbers. The first four numbers matched, and the last four were within the right range: A67034000, then 4004 and 4005.

"Sorry, those are stolen bills. They came right off the top of the stack. You remember who spent these twenties?"

"Sure do. I own this place, work the whole day, open to close. This hombre didn't look right when he came in. He had town clothes, but a well-worn range hat and cowboy boots that had seen their share of roundups.

"First he bought ten dollars worth of chips with a twenty, then he promptly lost his stake in ten minutes at a poker game. He rushed upstairs when Judy was free and gave her a twenty-dollar tip on top of the two-dollar fee, which she turned in. I split it with her. The guy spent another twenty on the way out to buy two bottles of whiskey at two dollars a throw."

"What did he look like? Did you hear a name or where he stayed here in town?"

"No name, no address. Don't need it when you pay cash. As I remember, he was five eleven or so, had a six-gun tied down low. Drank hard, but didn't get drunk. Judy said he was a wild man in bed. No scars on his face or hands. Brown hair, clean-shaven, looked fairly fit."

"If you see him again, get word to the sheriff immediately. Could be a big reward if he can lead us to the missing money."

"Yeah, I'll do that." He moved down the bar to a customer. Fargo followed him. "You said this guy was with Judy last night. Is she here?"

"Yeah, but it'll cost you three dollars."

"Not just to talk it won't." Fargo headed for the two women sitting on the stairs. The blonde grinned at him and flipped open her house coat, showing one bare breast. "Hey there, buckskin man, how about a quick poking before lunch?"

"Maybe, if you're Judy."

The blonde frowned and pointed at the smaller girl beside her, younger and with dark hair. Skye moved a chair, turned it backward and straddled it.

"Judy, you had a client last night who gave you a twenty-dollar tip. You know his name?"

Judy lifted her painted-on brows in mock surprise. "Like I'm supposed to remember every customer who gives me a twenty-buck tip?" She lost her poise and giggled. "Damn right I remember him. Gave me his first name right off. Said he was Clete, but I could call him Mr. Brady. He was a real pistol. I mean, four times in an hour. I wasn't all that busy. But four times in an hour is some kind of a man."

"Say where he was going today?"

"Nope, just that he had to be damn sure to get on the six o'clock train this morning. He in some kind of trouble?"

"Looks like it. He killed at least two men and stole twenty-six thousand dollars from the train."

"Yeah, he's in trouble," Judy said, "but he's still a big tipper."

Fargo walked out of the saloon. At least he had a name, but the body that went with it was probably long gone on the train east.

Across the street from the saloon, a rail-thin man in a brown suit and a black bowler stood in the shade of the hardware store and watched the man wearing buckskins. Dutch figured that the railroad detective had talked to the girls by now, but he couldn't learn much. What if he did? The shooters were far gone on the train east this morning. He had seen them board. So far the snooper had learned damned little. It would stay that way. If the buckskin-clad man came too close to any of the important facts about this little caper, it would be good-bye, buckskins. The snoopy man on the flashy horse would die neatly and quickly. Dutch had given the big man his word on that.

5

Fargo had walked up the street past two storefronts when an attractive lady spoke to him. She looked about thirty, medium height and blonde, wearing a conservative gingham dress and a small hat. She held a pad of paper and a pencil in her hands.

"Pardon me, but aren't you Skye Fargo, the Trailsman, who the railroad brought in to help with the robberies?" she asked.

"Yes, miss, I guess I am. I didn't catch your name."

"Oh, I'm Sarah Wellford. I run the *Sentinel*, Plainview's local newspaper." She smiled, and he liked the looks of it. Soft blue eyes to go with the blonde hair, a slender body with a small waist and full breasts.

"Is your inventory over?" she asked with a cute little grin that seem to light up her whole face.

"Sorry, didn't mean to stare. You're extremely attractive for a reporter."

"Thank you. Now, back to business. I'm doing a story on the train robbery. Biggest thing to hit our little town in five years. I talked to Mr. Mannington, and he gave me a running account of the robbery. He told me that you tracked the bandits and found their graves. Do you know who killed them?"

"You seem to have the whole story, Miss Sarah. No, I don't know who killed the two robbers, or where the money and the gold vanished to."

"Oh. Well, the sheriff told me you said you tracked two

43

men on horseback who may have killed the robbers. Did they come all the way back to town?"

"They were headed this way, but I couldn't be sure they came all the way here. It was at night."

"Could the killers still be in town?"

"Yes, or they might have left on any of five or six trains out of here."

"What about the registered mail? Did you find all of it where it had been ripped up in the woods?"

"I found all of it that was there."

"Was any missing?"

"You'll have to ask the post office inspector that."

"I did, he wouldn't tell me."

"So?"

"So I'd like to interview you about the way you tracked down the robbers, get all the details. What sign you found at the campfire. How you knew there was coffee there, and how you found the graves."

"Miss Wellford, can you set type?"

"Of course. How do you think I get the paper out every two weeks? I set type, write the stories, make up the headlines, check the page proofs, do the ads, and then run the press. Two small boys help me deliver the papers."

"Good, a real newspaper person. Now, I have some people to see this morning. Maybe we could talk over lunch. You do eat a noontime meal?"

"Yes, sure. Be glad to take you to lunch. How about at Bess's Diner at twelve-thirty?"

"That's fine."

"Good. Oh, do you always wear buckskins?"

"Yes. They keep me closer to mother earth and father sun."

"That's Indian kind of talk, isn't it?"

"Yes. See you for lunch." He touched his high-crowned gray cowboy hat as she turned away. She smiled again, and he liked the way it brightened her pretty face.

Fargo went to the train station to the room where they

had the registered mail. The inspector opened the door and ushered him in.

"We have all the registered back in sacks for delivery. The local sack has been taken to the post office. The rest waits for the train, all westbound to the end of the tracks."

"We have contacted some of those who had registered items we haven't found. Three of them are here in town. One is Kirk Gaylord, a local businessman. He's been over here three times checking. You might want to talk with him."

"He say what the missing item is?"

"No, only that it was terribly important. I'll give you the names of the other two locals with missing mail."

Ten minutes later, Fargo sat in Kirk Gaylord's office over the hardware store.

"It's absolutely vital that I get that package back," Gaylord said. "It's the only copy of my father's last will and testament. My guess is that getting that will might have been the main purpose of this robbery. Somebody knew it would be on board. Somebody hired those men to rob the train and take the will and destroy it, or take it to someone else."

"Who would do that, Mr. Gaylord?"

"My brother and my sister. Under the old will, each of us gets one point three million dollars, and the remainder of the estate is to be split evenly. My brother and sister hated our father. They ridiculed him and were mean to him the last two years of his life. He was well enough to realize this and changed his will two months before he died. The new will gives me three million dollars, and my siblings get a half million each. Any additional money left in the estate is mine."

"Your brother and sister would kill to get the will?"

"Yes, at least my brother would. It's a difference of eight hundred thousand dollars."

"Who knew the will was being sent by mail?"

"Only myself and my lawyer in St. Louis, who drew up

the will. My father died a week ago in St. Louis. My siblings knew about the changes in the will. There was only one signed copy, so just one legal copy. That's the one missing."

Fargo said he'd do what he could. He went to the next local person with a missing item from the registered mail. He knocked on the door of a small cottage at the edge of town. It was surrounded with wildflowers and petunias and hollyhocks in full bloom.

The door opened. "Hello, young man, I'm Mrs. Sadie Utley, what can I do for you today?"

Mrs. Utley was about sixty-five, spry, sharp and more than a little worried. He told her why he was there.

"Yes, tragic about those two young men who died. Even if they were the robbers, it wasn't right they should die. I'm terribly upset about the family Bible. It came from Chicago from my cousin. He said he'd send it registered mail so it would be safe. Who would steal an old tattered Bible?"

"That does seem strange, Mrs. Utley. We'll look into it and see what we can turn up. It definitely wasn't among the material I picked up in the woods."

"Oh, one more thing. Hidden in the back flap on the cover are three thousand-dollar bills. Somebody might have found the bills and then destroyed the Bible. I do truly want to get back that book. It contains the history of my family on the flyleaf that goes back six generations."

"We'll do the best we can to get your Bible back," Fargo promised.

The last local with missing mail was Ephraim Delano, who lived down the block from the courthouse. He answered the door. He was from sixty to seventy years old, had a limp when he walked, and wheezed with every breath. He hadn't shaved for a week, and his hair was white and uncombed.

"Mr. Delano, I'm with the railroad. Wanted to talk to you about your missing registered mail."

"About damn time somebody did. Come in, come in.

My brother sent me five thousand dollars in bearer bonds from St. Louis. Them are the ones that aren't registered and whoever has them, owns them. Sell them like cash money. No questions. Where the hell is my five thousand in bearer bonds?"

"We're looking into it, Mr. Delano. Something is bound to turn up. Tell your brother to hold on to his receipt that he sent them."

"I was gonna buy the Frontier Hotel and spend my last days in comfort, with no worries and good food. Now what the hell can I do? I don't have more than fifty dollars to my name and this ramshackle house."

"We'll do all we can for you, Mr. Delano." Fargo wished mightily that he hadn't taken this job. Now he was paying for that first lazy week of lying around the hotel.

Ten minutes later on Main Street, Fargo heard about the bloody murder. He got directions to the house from the barber. The sheriff was there and grunted when he saw Fargo.

"Robbery done after a murder," the sheriff said. "His money, watch, stickpin, even his shirt cuff links are all gone."

"Knife job," Fargo said. "Carotid. When the heart is pumping, they'll squirt blood for ten feet with every heartbeat. Sheriff, look at the man's boots. Those are hundred-dollar cowboy boots hand made in Taos, Mexico. Why would a thief pass up boots like that?" Nobody had an answer.

At twelve-thirty, Fargo walked into Bess's Diner, which the newspaper publisher had suggested, and found her waiting for him. She wore different clothes, a white blouse and a blue skirt. The blouse was snug across her breasts and the top button was open, showing just a hint of creamy cleavage.

She held out her hand. "Well, Mr. Skye Fargo. I've been hearing a lot of things about you. Turns out you are a rather famous character."

"Whatever you heard is wrong," Fargo said with a grin.

"If it's something bad about me, it's only half true. If it's something good, it's highly exaggerated."

She scribbled a note on her pad. "I'm going to quote you on that. Now, tell me about your being a trailsman, sniffing out the tracks of these killers and robbers. My readers want to know how you do it."

Fargo had been asked to tell this before. He told her about this particular trail on the railroad right-of-way, and briefly how he had followed it, the sign he found, the graves, and how he tracked the men west until the sun went down.

Sarah had been taking notes rapidly. She would get most of it right. She looked up, her blue eyes curious, her smile genuine. "You do this kind of tracking all over the western states and territories?"

"Yes, I tend to stay busy."

She leaned forward, and her white blouse fell open a little to show more of her luscious bosom. "It sounds like interesting work, but isn't it dangerous, too?"

"Usually, but not nearly as dangerous or exciting as sitting across the table from a beautiful lady trying to keep her talking just so I can be with her for a few more minutes."

Sarah blushed. "That, Mr. Fargo, is a wonderfully nice thing to say. I'm flattered and pleased. Now, if you ask me out to dinner, I'll be totally delighted."

"I'll be right here at seven for dinner tonight if the time is good for you. One of the great benefits of this work is all the wonderful people I get to meet." He touched her hand and felt a spark of electricity from her flushed skin. "Yes, I'll be here tonight. Now, if you'll excuse me, there's a man I need to talk to."

Sarah smiled and nodded. "Good. Until seven."

Two blocks from the restaurant, Marty Johnson lay halfway down an alley. He was drunk and sick. He shifted in the dirt next to a building and struggled to sit up against the clean clapboards. He made it and at once vomited. Half of it splashed on his filthy pants. Marty wiped his mouth, wishing he could pass out, but he didn't. How had he afforded all that booze?

He drifted a moment, but snapped back when he heard someone coming down the alley. When he looked that way, he lost his fragile balance and leaned over again into the dirt and vomit. His face was to the wall. If he didn't move, maybe they wouldn't kick him. He heard two voices, one plaintive, the other strong and commanding.

"Look, we agreed on the split, and it stands," the heavier voice said.

"The take was ten times what we figured," the whiny voice protested. "We just planned on the gold bars."

"We split that, the rest is mine, Dutch. If you don't like it, you go talk to Baldy Ingram over there in his house."

"Shit, you can't say that. We worked this one together. We need to split the whole thing. You couldn't have done this one without me."

The men were past him then, the voices fading. Marty shook his head and tried to sit up again, but instead he fell the other way. Phrases kept coming back to him: "split, my share, gold bars, Dutch." The words drummed into his head.

It was almost like when he had been a cop back in Philadelphia. Then he shot that suspect who was innocent and the guy died. Marty had turned in his badge. He hadn't had a good night's sleep since. He looked down the alley. Nobody coming. Marty passed out.

Four hours later, Marty came awake slowly. He hurt in half the bones in his body. Vomit tainted his mouth. He remembered the two guys arguing in the alley. The words they had used stuck in his brain: the split, my share, gold bars, and the name Dutch. Maybe he should tell the sheriff. No, he'd only kick him. Maybe this fancy tracker, the guy who wore buckskins. He'd heard about the train robbery. Was the buckskin guy working for the railroad?

Marty struggled to sit up, then to stand. He made it. He shuffled slowly down the alley, hoping he wouldn't be sick again. It took him ten minutes to walk to the end. He slumped there on the boardwalk next to the hardware store. He'd wait. The Trailsman would walk by sometime. Unfortunately, his willpower wasn't as strong as his sleep factor, and after ten minutes, he passed out again.

It was mid-afternoon before Marty came awake. Somebody kicked him where he lay on the boardwalk in the warm sunshine.

"Hey, easy. Don't do that."

"Marty, thought I told you to do your sleeping in the alley. You want me to lock you up again?"

Marty blinked through bleary eyes, got them in focus, and saw the sheriff standing over him. He sat up slowly.

"Sheriff, got to do something. Got to find the buckskin guy."

Sheriff Crosby snorted. "Why you need to see him? He's a busy guy with the railroad."

"Heard something. Need to talk to him."

"Talk to me, Marty. Known you a long time."

"Nope, got to talk to the Trailsman."

"His name is Skye Fargo. I see him, I'll send him to your office here."

"Thanks, Sheriff. I'm cutting down, did I tell you?"

"Sure, Marty. I'll send him around."

The 3:05 train pulled in from the east, and a dozen people got off before it took on two passengers and continued on west. The tracks went only as far as Springdale, the end of the line about twenty miles west.

Terrance Gaylord stepped off the train, looked around, and headed down Main Street toward the Butler Building, where his brother had his office over the hardware store. Terrance had been there before. Tension and anger rode on Kirk's younger brother's shoulders like a feral lion as he marched across the street and up the stairs to the second floor. He went in the door without knocking and stared hard at his brother, interrupting his conversation with a client about a land sale.

"Terrance, why are you here? The reading isn't for two days yet."

"Free country, brother. I can go anywhere I want to. So happens I wanted to come out here and check on that spurious will you say our father wrote just before he died."

"Not just before—" Kirk stopped. "Mr. Davis, would it be all right if we worked out the details on this tomorrow? Looks like I have a family crisis here I better take care of first."

The customer nodded and scurried out the door away from what he must have figured would soon be a knock-down family fight.

When the man was gone, Kirk turned on his brother with anger splintering from his eyes.

"How could you do it? How could you hire someone to rob the train to get the new will? I know you did it. No other reason to rob a train way out here. You arranged it and your hirelings killed three people. You have the blood of three innocent men on your hands, little brother."

Terrance frowned and shook his head. "I don't have the slightest idea what you're talking about. I came to try to persuade you not to have a reading of the new will. It isn't fair and you know it. Father was not himself the past year or so, and didn't realize how unfair the new will is."

"Bullshit, Terrance. He knew exactly what he was doing. He knew how you and our sister were out spending money like water, gallivanting all over the world. Neither of you have ever done a stick of honest work in your life. It's up to me to keep what's left of father's business together."

"You're the bullshit specialist, Kirk. You sling it around like you're a stable hand. You know the new will is totally unfair, cutting us off from more than half of our inheritance. I won't put up with it. I'll find a local attorney and contest the will if you try to enforce its provisions. And I'll win. Missouri is good about that. The state law is all about fairness and equal division of assets to heirs."

"Get out," Kirk bellowed. "I'm ashamed to call you a

member of the family. Ginger would be a lot better off if she didn't hang on your coattails. Get out and don't come back until the reading. It's in two days at three in the afternoon before Judge Bartholomew in division court."

"I'll be there."

"It won't make any difference."

Terrance lifted his hand to hit his brother, but backed off and stalked to the door. He slammed the door so hard behind him that the latch broke.

Outside, Terrance paused. There was a man he had to see who had a lot of explaining to do.

Fargo paced down the boardwalk, heading for the hardware store. He could use some of the new cleaning patches they had out now for rifles and pistols. Better than trying to find some lint-free cloth every time he cleaned his guns. He heard the train come in and turned just in time to stumble over something on the boardwalk. He caught himself and looked down at a man lying there, asleep or drunk, Fargo didn't know which.

"Hey," Marty yelped. He looked up. "Hey, you in the buckskins. Need to talk."

Fargo looked down at the man, who struggled to sit up. He made it and leaned against the hardware front wall.

"Need to talk?" Fargo asked.

"Yep, sit down here a minute."

Fargo grinned and sat on the boardwalk and leaned back against the building. "Nice view from down here."

"Heard two guys talking in the alley. I'm a drunk, they didn't pay me no mind."

Fargo relaxed against the wall. "Heard something?"

"Yep. I used to be a cop, back in Philly." He blinked rapidly and wiped wetness away from his eyes. "Yeah, my ears are still sharp. Two town guys talking about 'the split,' and one was demanding his share be bigger. The heavy voice said something about gold bars. Then he called the smaller one Dutch." Marty looked over at Fargo. "That all mean anything?"

Fargo sat up straighter when the gold bars were mentioned. "You sure you heard that right?"

"Right as rain. I might be a drunk, but I ain't stupid."

"I agree. What's your name?"

"Marty Johnson." He held out his hand.

"Skye Fargo." They shook.

"Figure it might be important. Looked like the two was arguing on the street, then came down the alley so nobody would hear them. They didn't pay me no mind."

"Remember what they looked like?"

"Kind of dark in there. One guy was smaller than the other. About all I remember."

"You know anybody called Dutch?"

"Nope. Been around here two years, don't recollect any Dutch guy."

Fargo stood. "Come on, Marty. There's something I want you to do for me."

"Yeah, what?"

"Stand up and come with me."

Five minutes later, Fargo pushed Marty into Milly's Bath House. He paid the twenty-five cents for Marty to take a bath, and gave the attendant three dollars to go buy Marty a new shirt and pair of pants. Then he headed for the sheriff's office.

"Haven't heard about Dutch for a year or so," Sheriff Crosby said when Fargo asked him. "He used to be around here. Sharp dresser, sneaky, would work for anybody. I knew he was a thief and burglar, but we could never catch him. He must be back in town. He's a real sidewinder."

"Like to have a talk with him," Fargo said.

"He used to do his drinking at the Roundhouse Saloon."

"Thanks, Sheriff."

There were only six men and one woman in the Roundhouse when Fargo walked in a few minutes later. He asked for a beer and talked to the apron. "Has Dutch been around today? I need to see him."

"Don't know any Dutch," the barkeep said.

"Sure you do. He does his drinking and gambling in here. Been away for a while but he's back in town. You see him today, tell him it's important I talk to him before dark. Got that?" Fargo slid a silver dollar across the bar. "Keep the change." He finished the beer and headed for the door.

"Hell, man, I'll tell Dutch if you got any more of them silver round ones."

Fargo looked at the man. He was slender, maybe thirty, wore a town hat and held a pitcher of beer.

"Tell him I need to see him," Fargo said, walked out the door, and hurried across the street. He leaned into the shadows near the barbershop and waited.

Five minutes later, the thin man in the town hat came out of the Roundhouse Saloon and looked both ways, then headed down the street at a fast walk. Fargo followed him from across the street. The man went down three doors and into a store that sold tinware, heating stoves, ranges, and boilers. Fargo waited several minutes, but the man didn't come out. He must have cut through the store to the rear alley and slipped away. Fargo was sure that Dutch would get the word that someone wanted to see him.

Fargo checked with the postal inspector at the depot. He had finished his work and waited for the next train east.

"We've tied down the six who lost material. We'll do what we can for them. Might have to settle some money. The man in Denver said his was not all that important. We hate to lose even one item from the registered mail. Hurts our reputation."

"If I dig up anything more, I'll send a wire to you in St. Louis," Fargo said. He took down the man's name and address, then checked his watch. The sun was either ten minutes late, or his new pocket watch was ten minutes fast. He bet on his watch. Four-fifteen. Lots of time before seven and dinner. He thought about Betty, the girl in the hotel. She was a big girl and could take care of herself. Besides, this was just a friendly dinner, no reason for Betty to get mad.

He headed for the stable to check on the Ovaro. The pinto got testy sometimes if left alone for too long. It was in the pasture, giving a mare a bad time with a nip here and there. It came at once to Fargo's whistle. It shook its black mane at Fargo, and its big eyes glinted with what Fargo figured was pleasure. A good ear scratch and neck rub was all Fargo could give it today. He slapped the stallion on the flank and sent it back to the fresh new grass in the newly opened pasture.

Fargo was on his way back to the hotel and just past the railroad station when he felt something pluck at his shoulder and then heard the shot. He dove to the ground, came up behind a water trough, and tried to figure where the shot came from. He felt his left shoulder. No blood, but the slug had torn a hole in his buckskins and a burn across the flesh. The depot was just across the street. He scanned the area and caught a glint of sun off steel, just as a second shot blasted from the depot and dug into the thick trough planks.

The sniper was forty yards away. Far out of range of Fargo's Colt. No cover between here and there. Fargo checked the other possibilities. He was on the far side of the street. A farm wagon was clattering down the dirt road. When it was opposite the depot and masking the shooter, Fargo ran out, ducked down behind the wagon, and ran along beside it to the far end of the depot, then sprinted in back of the building near the tracks.

The shooter must have moved by that time. Fargo worked up cautiously along the depot, past freight carts and stacks of boxes. When he looked around the far end of the depot, no one showed at the corner. He jogged down to the end and studied the ground. The boot prints were plain. He found two shell casings in the dust. Fargo stayed back six feet from the sign. He saw where the shooter had turned and then run. The toes had dug strongly into the soft dirt. He headed for the tracks and the houses across the way.

Fargo memorized the size and shape of the cowboy boot, then followed the faint footprints across the rails down the slope of the right-of-way and into the weeds and grass on the far side.

He hunkered down in a shallow ditch. There were three houses just ahead and no cover between Fargo and the houses. If the shooter was still watching, Fargo could be a dead duck. Test him. Fargo sprang up from the cover of the ditch and ran ten yards along the tracks, then dropped back into the cover. No shots sounded.

He surged out of the depression and sprinted for the first house, his Colt in hand. He made it to the back of the house, edged around the corner, and stormed to the front. No one there. He scanned the area and to the far left saw a rider on a roan horse three hundred yards away, charging into a patch of oak and hickory.

No rush now. Fargo knew the horse would leave a highway of tracks. He jogged back to the livery stable and whistled up the Ovaro. Five minutes later, he was mounted and riding toward the patch of oak trees where the rider had vanished.

At the edge of the trees, Fargo dismounted and checked for sign. He found the galloping prints of the horse quickly and followed them into the woods. There the prints slowed to a walk through the trees and brush. They took a direct path through the copse and out the far side. There the horse went into a canter, and it headed in a roundabout way to the north of town.

Here in the open, Fargo could follow the tracks from his mount. He rode along watching the hoofprints, angling ahead, making better time. When the tracks led in one obvious direction, he galloped forward for forty yards, then slowed and checked for the prints again. The third time he lost the trail and backtracked to where he saw the prints turn off into another large spread of oaks with some ash and maple in the mix. He entered the woods and dismounted to follow the trail.

Twice it went onto a rocky slant, and he had to circle around it to find the tracks on the far side. The rider was on a route that looked like it would eventually come back to town.

On a slight rise, Fargo found an open place, and he stopped and scanned the countryside ahead. There were two farms and what looked like a small cattle ranch. To the far left, toward town, he saw a single rider. The color of the horse faded into the browns and greens of the countryside. But Fargo knew it had to be the same roan he had seen the sniper riding.

Fargo played his hunch and cut across the arc, aiming ahead of the other rider. He rode hard for a mile, then eased the Ovaro to a canter.

The other rider was still walking his mount. He must feel safe, Fargo mused. If he kept at a walk, Fargo would cut him off a mile from town in an open area. He kicked the Ovaro into another gallop for a quarter of a mile, then eased off. There was plenty of time. He looked at the sun. It was edging the far horizon. Another hour and a half of daylight should be enough.

A half hour later, he sat on the Ovaro just inside a small patch of elm and sweet gum near where the shooter would pass. Fargo remembered the long gun and knew he would have to surprise the man close enough to be in pistol range. That meant no farther than fifty feet. He judged the distances. The rider's path had been aimed at town. He had been skirting any patches of trees, and probably would go around this one as well. He was still a quarter of a mile away. Fargo could see the man turn and look back over his shoulder and along his back trail.

Fargo waited. A pheasant rocketed out of some grass near the shooter's path, and his horse shied, then settled back on track. The man looked behind again, then at the patch of woods. He hesitated, then took off his town hat and mopped his forehead. At the last moment he turned his mount toward the trees. Fargo grinned, at last a break. Maybe the rider wanted to get out of the hot sun for a minute. The sniper also sat hip-shot on the saddle, as if he wasn't used to riding. Fargo faded back in the brush and trees, dismounted, and moved toward where he figured the rider would enter the woods. He slid behind a thick trunk of a huge maple tree and waited.

Fargo spotted the horse and rider coming into the woods. The shooter ducked under a branch, and then stopped the horse, and looked round. He swung off the mount and limped around, then rubbed his inner thighs and his buttocks. They must hurt. Fargo could tell the sniper wasn't much of a trail rider. Fargo stayed behind the large maple tree but something gave him away. A moment later the bushwhacker fired three pistol shots under the horse at the tree where Fargo hid. He didn't return the fire. He listened. Years in the wilderness had helped him develop an acute sense of hearing. Fargo picked up the stealthy footsteps as the man hurried away using the horse as a shield.

A Sharps Old Reliable cavalry carbine rested in the sniper's saddle boot. Fargo moved silently up to the horse, grabbed the carbine, and rushed to the big maple that had shielded the shooter. He was gone. Fargo listened. The fugitive was too far away. An occasional branch snapped but not enough to determine distance. Fargo looked at the forest floor and found the marks the rider's boots had left: bent-down shoots of new grass and scuff marks in the mulch. They pointed out the way of the sniper's retreat. He moved forward, finding the small indicators that showed where the man had moved.

The tracks led to the edge of the woods, and just across from it was another section of forested land that stretched for four or five miles up a gradual slope. Fargo looked at the tracks. The toes of the man's boots had dug hard into the soft earth. He had run quickly across the open stretch of fifty yards. Fargo had the advantage now with the long gun. He jogged across, following the scuff marks in the short grass and weeds. He didn't go straight into the brush where he saw the tracks leading. Instead, fifty feet out he angled to the side so if the shooter planned to ambush him, there would be no chance.

Once in the brush, Fargo stopped and listened. A tracker had to move slower than the subject, so he wouldn't lose the trail. But Fargo didn't think this one would run that far. He would go to a spot where he thought he had an advantage and try to bushwhack Fargo as he moved up the trail.

The spot was closer than Fargo thought. He came to a steep ravine that was twenty feet deep with sloping sides. Heavy growth of hickory and elm covered the top of the far side. Fargo would have to move slowly down the side and then work back up the far slope. With the thick brush it was an ideal bushwhacking spot. He paused well back in the cover on his side. The slash through the hill was three or four hundred yards each way. Too long to go around. He settled down and watched the far side of the ravine.

Slowly, without rustling a leaf or branch, he wormed his way on the ground toward the front of the drop-off. Fargo burrowed under some flowering hawthorne and moved a small branch so he could see out perfectly yet remain hidden.

He lay there for ten minutes, scanning the area across from him. One particularly heavy copse of hickory caught his attention. It was about ten feet to one side of the direct access route. He watched it resolutely. Yes, a leaf moved. Again, a small branch trembled as if something had brushed past it. Fargo brought up the Colt and held his hand over the weapon as he cocked it, to hush the sound, then fired four quick shots into the brush where he saw it move. At once he rolled away from his shooting spot and huddled behind a gum tree trunk. One shot came back, then one more.

Fargo listened. All of the insects and birds in the woods went silent. In the void came a soft keening sound of a man in pain.

"You're shot, bushwhacker, and you're in pain. I can put five more rounds into you right there, and kill you. Or you can throw out your six-gun and slide gently into the gully right in front of you. Do you understand?"

"Go fuck a dog, Fargo, you bastard," the shooter said, and fired three times at the location of Fargo's voice. One of the rounds hit the tree that protected Fargo. He leaned around, found an opening, and fired his reloaded six-gun five times into the brush where he had shot before.

"Not so much fun when the target shoots back at you, is it, you yellow-bellied bushwhacker?"

Silence.

Fargo waited. He knew this new game. The shooter in the brush had been hit once or twice, or he was playing possum and not wounded at all, just waiting his chance.

Fargo moved silently up the woods beside the gully where it narrowed. Just around a slight curve where he couldn't see the shooter's position, Fargo crossed the gully. Then he began his best quiet movement through the light brush and gum and maple trees.

To cover fifty yards took several cautious minutes. When he figured he was twenty yards from the gunman, he stopped and listened. He soon heard a soft mumbling of words ahead. The man might have taken a bullet in a leg so he couldn't move.

Fargo held his cocked Colt in his right hand as he crawled forward without a whisper of a leaf. Another ten feet and Fargo could see him. He had his hat off, one arm was bloody, and his leg was twisted unnaturally under him. He leaned back against a gum tree, his face showing his pain.

Fargo fired one shot an inch over the man's head. The sound of the round going off in the brush was twice as loud as usual. The bushwhacker jumped; then his hand went down toward his revolver.

"Don't touch it or you're dead," Fargo thundered. The man's hand stopped moving. "Both hands on top of your head, now," Fargo ordered.

The man put up one hand and slowly moved the blood-ied hand up as well. Fargo ran into the spot and kicked away the pistol, then stared at the hatless man. He'd never seen him before.

"Who the hell are you, and why did you try to kill me?"

"Just . . . don't know, now. Seemed like some easy money."

Fargo grabbed the man's unwounded arm and twisted it behind the man's back and lifted it up until the man screeched in pain.

"Talk," Fargo demanded.

"Hell, I didn't even know you was following me. Name's Joe Downs."

"Who hired you to kill me?"

"Don't know. Got a letter in St. Louis with a hundred dollars in it. It said if I shoot you in Plainview today, I get another three hundred."

"Who sent the letter?"

"Don't know. Just an address in St. Louis to go to collect when you're dead."

Fargo swore. The man was telling the truth. He'd questioned enough men like this to know.

"Don't like people shooting at me, Joe. You're lucky to be alive."

"You done tracked me good. How you do that?"

"Practice, Joe. You're lucky to still be talking. Can you stand up on that leg?"

"Can't. Tried for ten minutes."

"I'll help you get on your horse, then we're going back to Plainview and straight to jail. I'm charging you with attempted murder. You won't have to worry about your room and board for the next ten years."

Fargo didn't bother to tie up the shot-up leg or shoulder. "You bleed to death on the ride back, your own damn fault. Tie them up anyway you can. Then we're riding out of this place."

The sun dipped beyond the rolling hills, and it was dark before they rode into Plainview to the sheriff's office. Just as he stepped down from the Ovaro, he remembered his dinner date. Fargo checked his store-bought watch. Seven-thirty.

"Now I am mad, Joe. You made me late for an important meeting."

Inside the lawman's office he found Sarah waiting for him.

"How did you know?" he asked before she said a word.

"Skye, I'm a reporter. Heard about the bushwhacking and saw you ride out of town. Figured you'd catch the shooter and bring him back here. Hurry up with the sheriff, I'm starved."

6

Dinner went well. Fargo washed up in the jail bathroom and even combed his dark hair before he put back on his wide-brimmed hat. He didn't take it off during the meal.

Sarah looked quizzically at his hat still in place. He explained.

"Bad habit I picked up from the Mountain Men and the cowboys. Never know when you might have to scoot or shoot, so you keep your hat on to save time reaching for it. Since most cowhands eat out on the prairie somewhere in the open, the hat keeps the sun from frying their heads."

Sarah scribbled as he talked. "Is that going in the story, too? You figure on filling up your whole paper with the train robbery?"

"Thought that I might." She smiled brightly, and Fargo admired her sunny countenance. "This is the biggest story to hit town in the five years that I've been here. So I'm going to do it up right."

"How did you become publisher of a newspaper at such a tender age?"

"Tender age? I'll have you know that I'm . . ." She paused. "Bad trick. A lady never mentions her age. I wouldn't either if I was anything but twenty-five, and an old maid by local standards. How? My daddy owned the paper. One day he slumped over at the type tray, had himself a heart attack, the doctor said. We buried him the next day. We didn't miss a single issue. Haven't since."

"You also have had some schooling, I'd bet."

"My daddy sent me to school in St. Louis. We lived nearby and he worked at a newspaper there." She stopped. "Mr. Fargo, I'm supposed to be interviewing you, not the other way around."

"Sorry, I tend to do that. Dessert? Oh, I did it again." She laughed and Fargo was fascinated with this well-proportioned lady with the beautiful face and a happy nature.

After dessert they talked over coffee, and it was nearly nine o'clock before they left. He insisted on walking her home.

"That's quite nice of you, Mr. Fargo, but I'm not going home. I have work to do at the paper. We're due out next Thursday, and I haven't even started writing the editorial page."

"Hey, maybe I could help."

She thought about it a moment, hand on her chin. Then she grinned and shook her head. "I don't think so. I make enough typos as it is, and with you there flustering me . . ."

"I promise not to fluster."

He walked her to the small newspaper building beside the bank, where she went inside, waved, and locked the door behind her. Fargo shrugged and headed back to his hotel.

In the room, Betty didn't believe he'd been working or that someone had shot at him.

"Absolutely true. Now, I have to go out to the saloons and try to find some man named Dutch."

"I want to come."

"Betty, respectable women don't go into saloons."

"Oh, right. Bet they have fancy women in there. I've never even seen a fancy woman, let alone talked to one. How are they different from other women?" She blushed. "I—I mean, do they look different? What?"

"Most of them are simply women who are down on their luck and have no other way to make a living. As a group they are not a happy bunch of ladies."

"Oh. Maybe I should read some more on my copy of Shakespeare. I'm trying to understand *Macbeth*."

Fargo told her that was a good idea and slipped out the door. His first stop was at the Plainsman Saloon. It was a rundown booze bucket with a grouch behind the bar, four tables for card playing, and one girl who, if she was in the right mood, would unload the lead from your pencil upstairs. Fargo talked to four of the six men there. Most of them didn't know Dutch. One man said Dutch used to be in town but he had left.

The third saloon was the Roundhouse, where Dutch used to spend his drinking time. This was a better class of establishment, with ten card tables, a long bar, and even two booths in the rear.

"I'm looking for a man named Dutch," Fargo told the bartender, a different one from the man he had seen before.

"Never heard of him," the apron said, his face a blank stare.

"Strange, this is his favorite saloon."

Fargo interrupted four card games to ask the same question, but none of the men said they had seen anyone named Dutch.

When Fargo left the bar, Dutch, still wearing his brown suit and black bowler, eased away from a card game thirty dollars richer and slipped out the side door. He hurried into the night.

Five minutes later, Dutch opened a Hallmark Hotel room door and walked into near darkness. One candle burned on the dresser and gave off a reluctant glow. A man sat in a chair smoking a cigar.

"So what's so important?" the shadowy man asked.

"I just saw this buckskin guy, Fargo, asking around for me. He went to all the saloons in town asking if anyone knew where I was."

"Interesting. Now, I wonder why he would do that?"

"He must know something. You hear anything? What does the sheriff know? What the hell are we going to do?"

"First you're going to settle down, Dutch. The sheriff knows nothing. We covered our tracks. Not a thing can go wrong. Maybe you should take a vacation. Go to Chicago. Spend some of your money back there. I advanced you three hundred dollars."

"Yeah, right. But I don't like the idea of this Fargo going around asking about me. He must know something."

"Relax, Dutch, just relax."

"Maybe it would be good to just eliminate him. I can cut him good with my blade. He's got to bleed like other men. Never was much with a revolver. But my blade, that little sweetheart I can make talk, and it knows Fargo's name."

"No, absolutely not. You kill him and the whole thing explodes. Everyone knows he's looking for you. Then he gets cut into hog meat, and everyone knows who did it. Not a chance. Forget about it, Dutch. Go back to the saloon and have two girls at once. An all-nighter always settles you down."

"Shit, maybe you're right. Just hang tough. Yeah, I'll try."

"Dutch, we do have one small problem. I received a telegram today from St. Louis. The 'merchandise' was not delivered. The guy just never showed up with it. Our man there says he has to have it in two days or we're in deep trouble."

"Nate Frazer knew how important it was to get that package to the right person," Dutch said. "What in hell happened?"

"I gave it to him myself," the man in the chair said. "He had plenty of time to make the train. He should have been there early this morning."

"So I better find Frazer. He's a dead man if he fucked up. I know where he hangs out."

"Without that package, we don't collect our fifty thousand dollars. This is a fifty-fifty split, remember." The man blew out a mouthful of smoke. "Find that bastard and see what happened."

Fargo finished talking to the men at the fourth and last saloon in the small town and headed back to the hotel. Nothing. He had come up against a blank wall. If Dutch had been at one of the saloons, he hadn't spoken up. Maybe anyone in town who knew him was too frightened to speak up. The man must be deadly.

Betty was sleeping when he unlocked the hotel room and went inside. He undressed and slid into bed beside her. She didn't wake up. At least he'd get a good night's sleep.

The next morning's breakfast with Betty was quick and quiet. She was mad about something, and Fargo could guess that it was because he was working and not spending all day with her. Couldn't be helped.

He knocked on the bank door at nine. He knew it didn't open until ten, but the banker saw him and came out.

"We don't open for an hour," Vernon Zilke said.

"I'm not banking. Wonder if you found any of those twenty-dollar bills that were stolen. The ones with the serial numbers we gave you."

"Oh, that. Yes, I meant to find you yesterday afternoon. Come in. We did take in one of the stolen bills. The clerk at the window didn't check the number, but he remembered who turned it in. Greg Mossler over at the general store."

"Tell the sheriff, he'll pick it up. Mossler will have to take the twenty-dollar loss. I need to talk to him right away."

Greg Mossler had a broom sweeping down the boardwalk in front of his store. The boardwalk was a foot off the street level and kept some of the dirt from the street out of the store. Each firm built its own walk in front, and sometimes they didn't match level and even.

Fargo watched the store man sweep a moment before he noticed the visitor.

"Mr. Mossler?"

"Right as chilblains in winter, what can I get for you?"

"Some information. You deposited a twenty-dollar bill yesterday at the bank. Turns out it was one of those stolen from the train couple of days ago."

"Damn, then I lose myself twenty dollars."

"Afraid so. Can you tell me who passed it to you yesterday?"

"Well, now, that won't be too hard. I don't get many. My wife helps me sometimes, and she took it in. I had one twenty that I checked, and it wasn't on the list. She said some kid spent it. Don't know the boy, neither did she. Said he was about five feet tall, well dressed, had blond hair, and pimples all over his face. About fourteen, she said, sassy and smart-alec, a real pain. He bought a new jackknife for eighty-five cents, wife told me. Then he wanted the change all in one-dollar bills.

"Now, we're fairly new in town, so we don't know everyone yet. But I don't remember seeing this kid before from what the wife said. Neither did she. If he comes in with another of those brand-new bills, I'll check the number and then grab him and send for the sheriff."

Fargo thanked him and headed back toward the small county courthouse.

Down the street at the bank, Ephraim Delano shuffled along the boardwalk to the bank door and pulled at it. Locked. The owner of the bank saw him and let him in, then locked the door behind him.

"Yes, Mr. Delano, what can we do for you today?"

"Want to borrow that five thousand dollars we talked about. Got to buy that hotel."

"You were waiting for those bearer bonds from your brother, you told me. Did they come in?"

"Nope, still missing. Damned railroad robber got them. Can I still borrow another five thousand without them?"

"That's a whole different story. You told me you have no collateral. With the five thousand missing, we can't advance you even a hundred dollars."

"Can't do it, or you just being miserable and mean and won't?"

"One or the other. But I can't take that kind of risk."

Ephraim sat there in the chair by the bank president's desk and shook his head. "Hell, just like I thought. An old man with no cash ain't a good credit risk. Figured. Well, I better get on back home and figure out a good way to die. About all that I got left."

Zilke winced. "Now, Mr. Delano, the railroad tells me that they have a good chance of finding the money and your bonds. Just give us a week or so, and then we'll talk again. You don't go and do anything foolish."

"Yep, I hear, young feller. You give out free advice, but don't lend no money. I hear."

He stood with an effort and walked slowly to the front door of the bank, then shuffled out the unlocked door. He turned and looked at the banker.

"Next week? You said give you a week. I'll be back here next week to talk to you."

The banker closed the door gently and locked it. He held up his hands. There was nothing else he could do.

Nate Frazer sat on the train grinding along the tracks west heading for Plainview, which was still thirty miles away. He had left town on an eastbound train early yesterday morning after waking up in a hotel room and realizing that he didn't have the package he was being paid two hundred dollars to deliver to St. Louis.

He had panicked. All he could think of was to get away from the people he knew would kill him if he stayed in town and didn't have the goods. Yes, he had been stupid. How could he have lost it?

It all began when a man he knew only slightly asked him if he would make a delivery of some important papers to an address in St. Louis. They would give him the package that night, and he was to get on the 6:05 train and deliver it that afternoon in St. Louis. He said he was out of work and would be glad to make the run.

The man gave him a hundred dollars and said he'd get the rest from the man in St. Louis. Sounded fair. Then he got curious. Why would they give him two hundred dollars to deliver a package? It must be worth a hell of a lot more than that. He'd take a quick look at the package. It wasn't big or heavy. Just an envelope with some papers inside. He looked at it and saw writing and the word *will* and the large figures, and he understood. It was a will that covered almost four million dollars. Yeah, he could keep the damned will and sell it back to them for, say, fifty thousand dollars. He would be rich.

So he celebrated. He bought a bottle at some saloon and got so drunk he couldn't see straight. He remembered some little whore, but he didn't know who she was. He had spent half the day yesterday morning trying to retrace his steps. One barkeep remembered him, but said he didn't stay in that saloon long. He wound up totally confused and getting more frightened all the time.

They would kill him. He knew they would. That man who gave him the package made it clear he would be in big trouble if he didn't get the goods delivered. He didn't take the train in the morning. By noon he was so scared he ran to the depot and just made the one o'clock heading for St. Louis. He wanted to get as far away as he could from Plainview.

Fifty miles down the tracks he left the train and tried to think it through. He took a hotel room and had a good meal and thought about the situation again. He had to go back and find that package, the envelope with the will inside. That morning he had taken the train heading for Plainview. When he got there, he had to find the package.

That afternoon Terrance Gaylord picked up a telegram from his contact in St. Louis. The package had not been delivered on time. He'd wait an hour and send another wire.

Terrance found Dutch in the boardinghouse where he lived, and they walked down the street.

"The package didn't get there," Gaylord said.

"What do you mean? I gave it to the guy. He said he'd be on the train yesterday morning at six-oh-five."

"All I know is that the package didn't get to my lawyer's office in St. Louis. You find that package and you give it to me before that damned judge calls for the reading, or you're a dead man. My gun is faster than your knife, Dutch, believe it."

Dutch waved his arms. "How could it go wrong? I trust that kid I hired to do the job. Know him well. How could he fail?"

"He did. We're talking about eight hundred thousand dollars here, Dutch. You know how much money that is? What did you make last year, three hundred dollars, maybe five hundred? Think about eight hundred *thousand* dollars."

"Mr. Gaylord, I don't know what to say."

"Don't say anything, Dutch. Get out in the street and find that man and that package, or I'll squash you like a dirty little bug on the boardwalk."

Fargo had word from the sheriff's office that another merchant had taken in one of the stolen twenties. Fargo went to see the leather maker, who did saddles, harnesses, and had a line of costly boots. Fargo loved the smell of a leather shop. Something about the tanned cowhides turned him into a little boy again dreaming of the Wild West.

Jim Drager scowled as he told Fargo about it. He was about forty, tanned, fit, and wore a leather apron with pockets in it for his tools. He came away from a half-finished saddle and shook his head.

"I never should have talked to that snot-nosed kid. Should have run him out of the store. He's been around before mooning over some cowboy boots. Then he flashed the twenty and I crumbled. I ain't seen a twenty for two months."

"The kid, was he about fourteen?"

"Yeah, how did you know? Had pimples and sores all over his face. Made him look weird. He said he wanted the most expensive pair of boots I sell. They go for fifteen dollars. Now I'm out the boots and the twenty. Damn."

"You said you'd seen him before. Know his name?"

"No, but I thought my wife might. She's in back. When I told her about him, she said maybe we've seen him at church. I described him for her, and she said no chance. The boy in church is the same age with blond hair, but his face is clear. We don't know who this one is."

Fargo thanked the man and left. School. The kid would have to go to school. He asked around and found out that the teacher was working this summer at Farm Home Café. That was his next stop.

The teacher was tall and thin with a severe face and clothes to match. Her dress dragged the floor and covered her to the wrists, with a ruffle under her chin.

"A fourteen-year-old boy with blond hair and his face a mass of pimples? No, not in my school. We have quite a few children, but not a lot at that age. It goes in waves, the number of children at each age. Right now there are only four fourteen-year-olds in the whole school. But no boy anywhere near like that one you describe."

Fargo thanked her and left, not sure where to check next. He headed down the boardwalk toward the sheriff's office again. It seemed he was there five or six times a day. He'd tell the sheriff what he had found out so far.

Before he got there, Fargo saw Kirk Gaylord come down the steps from his office and turn toward the bank. He was thirty feet ahead of Fargo. Gaylord passed the alley and was about to turn into the bank when a man popped out of the alley and fired four times with a handgun at Kirk's broad back.

Fargo saw it all. He charged forward, his hand loosening the Colt in his own leather. A woman with two toddlers came toward him. He tried to go around them. One small

72

boy staggered the wrong way at the wrong time, and Fargo brushed him and in the process lost his balance and fell hard on the planks. He jumped up, picked up the toddler, and gave him to his mother, then charged into the alley.

It was empty. He ran down the hundred feet to the cross street and looked both ways. Nothing. No human moving in either direction. *Wait,* he told himself, *steady down and observe.* He heard no doors slam, saw no one suddenly leave a house. There were four houses on the street in back of the business firms. He saw that two had small pastures behind them. He walked that way. He holstered his weapon, and watched and listened.

A horse whinnied. Another horse answered it. Then he ran forward until he could see between the houses and the pastures.

A rider had just come out the gate at the second house, seen Fargo, and turned and galloped off in the other direction toward a heavy stand of hardwood trees a quarter of a mile in back of the house.

Fargo ran for the second house, found a horse with halter and bridle tied by the back door. A saddle lay on the ground near it. He grabbed the reins, pulled them loose, and vaulted onto the horse. A woman came out of the back door and yelled.

"I'm with the sheriff, need to borrow your horse." Then he was gone, feeling like an Indian, riding bareback toward the woods. He could just spot the other rider on a bay vanishing into the brush and trees. At that distance Fargo couldn't tell if there was a rifle on the saddle or not. His guess would be there wasn't.

Fargo knew the mount he had was a short horse. Great stamina, fastest horse alive for a quarter of a mile, big rear quarters and lots of staying power. He galloped the mare halfway to the woods, then trotted her to a spot fifty feet from where the other rider entered the brush. He wasn't going to be bushwhacked again. He moved up cautiously to the place where the other horse had entered and found the trail of the horse. It was easy to follow. The trees included lots of short-leaf pine and not much underbrush. The patch of woods was about ten acres, and the trail soon led out of it and angled to the west.

Where was this back-shooter heading? Fargo tried to remember if Kirk Gaylord had fallen after the shots. He had been concentrating on the gunman. He thought back over it again, and he remembered a glimpse of Gaylord going down to his left. Had he been hit or was he dodging the bullets? No, he had no way of knowing that someone would shoot at him. He must have been hit. Fargo wondered how bad.

Fargo edged out of the woods and spotted the rider a half mile ahead. If he rode the mount that hard for two more miles, it would founder and go down with laminitis. Then he'd be walking. The country ahead was full of rolling hills, with a few flat places. The wooded areas were mostly behind them. For several miles ahead it was a straight chase through the open country.

Fargo slowed his mount to a walk and tried to remember how he used to ride bareback with the Indian tribe that had befriended him one summer when he was fourteen. He couldn't. Ahead, the rider went over a small rise and down out of sight. Fargo had an urge to speed up, but he didn't. The horse needed a rest, and the shooter ahead couldn't find any spot along here for an ambush.

When Fargo topped the rise ten minutes later, he saw the rider the same distance ahead, walking his mount. The shooter must have planned the attack, and the getaway. He'd had the horse saddled and ready. Then why hadn't he taken a rifle with him? Maybe he had. The rider turned more west now and angled toward a good-size wooded area.

Fargo wanted to close the gap before the shooter made it to the woods. He kicked the mare in the flanks, and she broke into a gallop that left Fargo gripping the animal with his legs, hoping he could stay on her back. They traveled two hundred yards and had just come to a flat area before the woods when the mare stumbled, one leg sank a foot into a gopher hole, and she went down. Fargo flew over her head and landed on his shoulder, rolling to lessen the impact.

The horse lay on her side, one leg bent back at a right angle with a splintered leg bone sticking through the flesh. The mare screamed with a sound that only a horse can make when it is in terrible pain or fearful for its life.

Fargo sat up and rubbed his bruised shoulder, then went to the horse. Its big brown eyes pleaded with him, and she screamed again. There was no way to save the horse. Fargo took out his Colt and fired one shot into her head, killing her instantly. He sat on the ground beside her and brushed his hand across his eyes. He hated to see animals suffer, and he hated even more having to put a good horse like this one out of its misery.

He stood and assessed his situation. He unbuckled his gun belt and slung it over his shoulder like a bandoleer and buckled it across his chest. He carried the Colt six-gun in his right hand. He began trotting toward the woods.

He'd learned a long-distance pace when he was with the Indians. A good Indian brave could outdistance a man on a horse over a day's time. Most of a rider's time on a horse was spent walking at four miles an hour. A Crow brave could do a ground-eating trot that would devour six miles an hour. The Indian would have only his bow, knife, and six arrows. Fargo had wrapped his gun belt around his chest so the holsters wouldn't flap against his legs.

Fargo settled into a five-mile-an-hour pace as he ran across the rolling Missouri countryside. It wasn't a sure thing. He should be able to keep up with the man on the horse, but perhaps not catch him. It would be a good contest. He saw the rider vanish into the woods.

The forest would give Fargo the advantage. He could maintain his pace, but the horse would have to slow down to negotiate through the brush.

A half hour later, Fargo was sweating. He checked the hoof prints on the forest floor. The rider was walking his mount again and seemed to be keeping near the side of the wooded area. As he jogged along on his pace, Fargo adjusted the gun belt around his shoulders and kept running.

The tracks became confused for a moment. The man had stopped and turned the animal around, evidently checking his back trail. Then he moved forward, moving faster across an open area before he returned to a walk in the denser brush. As Fargo ran along the trail, he wondered if the man ahead had lost his way in the tangled forest.

Tucker Albright had planned it carefully. He had got the job last night, and had time to check on the target. He was told that the man he wanted went to the bank every day just before it closed at three. He knew the route, had walked through the alley, and had his horse ready to ride. How could he fail?

He had no idea where the man chasing him had come from. Suddenly he was there shouting at him. He raced through the alley to the horse and rode. Soon he saw the man behind him, taking the neighbor's horse and riding hard. Maybe at last he had lost the guy. He checked behind twice and didn't see the horse anywhere.

If he'd been watching closer, he might have noticed the hesitation of his own horse. He kicked the animal in the flanks, and she stepped ahead, then shied and whinnied, rearing straight up on her hind legs. Tucker Albright wasn't ready for it. He was a fair rider, but this sudden move caught him with his toes barely in the stirrups. He fell off backward, wildly waving his arms and twisting so he wouldn't land on his back. When he came down, he hit hard on his hands and knees, then painfully rolled over on his back.

The mare had come down but was still stomping her front feet on the ground, working gradually backward. Tucker spotted the problem. A four-foot rattlesnake, one of the deadly Massa variety, had struck the mare's lower leg. The snake lashed out and struck again, sinking fangs into the tender flesh and withdrawing. Before the horse could back up enough, it struck again. This time the mare came down with her shod front hooves squarely on the coil of the rattler. The force of the horse's weight sliced off the rattler's head while the tail kept on rattling.

The horse pranced away a few yards and pawed with her hooves as if her front legs hurt. Did rattlesnake bites affect horses? Tucker didn't know. He caught the mare, stepped back into the saddle, and rode her hard through the woods for a quarter of a mile. Then the mare slowed, went down hard on her front legs, and rolled over, throwing Tucker off. He landed on his feet. The mare screamed. The death scream came softer and softer. Moments after she went down the mare's big head came up, then fell hard into the mulch of the woods floor.

Tucker stared at the dead horse for a minute, then walked to the west and north. He had to get back to town and get the train out of there. Sure as shit the guy behind was going to keep looking for him. He wasn't even sure if he had killed that guy in town. If he hadn't, he couldn't collect any more money. Tucker walked faster, wondering when the rider behind him would catch up. He had done every trick he knew of to throw the rider off his trail except circling around him, and he didn't have time for that. Now he picked the hardest ground and rocky areas he could find to hike over. That should slow down the rider chasing him.

Less than a half-mile behind Tucker, Fargo kept up his trot. He'd seen his Indian friends maintain this pace for six hours before stopping to rest for ten minutes, then going another six hours.

From time to time he stopped and examined the hoof prints of the bushwhacker's horse. He was closing the gap. The weeds and grass the horseshoes bent over were not coming up as fast. He was closer to the animal that made the prints.

A short time later he saw a form ahead, and he stopped and dodged behind a tree. He saw the horse he had been following, but it was lying down in an unnatural position. Had it foundered? Was it sick? Fargo moved up cautiously. Then he saw the swollen front legs. He'd experienced this problem before. It could only be the result of several rattlesnake strikes. The horse could have been saved if it had been stopped and given minimal treatment. Running a horse in that condition would speed the poison to the heart and cause a quick and painful death.

Fargo nodded. Now the real contest began. They both were on foot miles from Plainview. Fargo took the gun belt off his shoulders and buckled it around his waist. Now the gunman ahead would find out why he was called the Trailsman.

7

Fargo stopped and retied his holsters tightly to his legs, then took out both Colts and held them in his hands. Then he picked up his pace to an easy run. He could cover a mile in eight minutes. The man ahead of him would be walking at no more than three miles an hour, unless he was tremendously fit, and probably scared to death.

With the first good boot prints in the grass, Fargo studied the sign. They were not cowboy boots, more likely farm boots, with a broad heel and sole. The grass lifted less from where it had been tramped down. He was gaining.

Fargo watched the trail critically. He was in the deep woods again, and the chance of an ambush was ever present. In thick brush he worked around it. In the clearer areas, he pushed a little harder. Once he stopped and listened. He could hear the faint sounds ahead of someone crashing through the brush.

Fargo continued to slip through the trees as the Indians did, brushing past, slipping under branches, not challenging them or trying to break them down. After another five hundred yards, he stopped and listened again.

Yes, the sounds were closer this time. As he waited, the sounds from ahead suddenly stopped. Why? Was the sniper resting, or he was working on a trap, an ambush? He must still have at least the pistol he used against the businessman in town. Fargo knew he didn't have a rifle. There had been no scabbard on the saddle.

Fargo couldn't tell for sure how far ahead the man was.

His guess was that he was within a hundred yards. This called for a new strategy. He slowed to a walk, making sure that he didn't break a twig or make any other noise. He seemed to float through the oak and hickory and sweet gum. The movements looked easy, but it had taken Fargo many years to perfect them.

He cocked his right-fisted Colt and walked forward cautiously, then stopped and didn't move as he listened. Fargo figured he was about twenty yards from the sounds of the man struggling.

Fargo moved ahead, more careful than ever about not making a sound. He angled in from the side, crawling slowly on the ground. He stopped, pushed aside some tall grass, and looked out. The man was crouched behind a big maple, his six gun aimed at his back trail. He had protection from that angle, but not from this side.

Fargo lifted his cocked Colt and aimed at the gunman's chest. The sniper had leaned around the tree to sight in on his trail behind.

"Move a muscle and you're a dead man," Fargo barked.

The man jumped, tried to swing his gun around, but the tree was in the way. Fargo fired. His first round hit the man in the left shoulder and knocked him sideways to the ground. He lifted up and fired his six-gun just after Fargo got off his second shot. Fargo's round took the bushwhacker hard in the chest and dumped him over backward where he lay. The bullet he fired nicked the tree Fargo had used for his protection and ricocheted into the brush.

Fargo waited. The man didn't move. Playing possum? Fargo moved quickly from tree to tree until he was ten feet from the man. The sniper lay on his back, his eyes wide open, staring at the tops of the trees. A dark stain showed on his pants where his bowels had emptied when he died.

The Trailsman took the man's weapon, plus a purse from his pocket. Inside he found a letter with the gunman's name and an address in St. Louis. He put them in his own pocket to turn in to the sheriff, and walked out of the woods. For a moment he scanned the sky, trying to orient himself.

Far off to the east and north he saw smudges in the sky that could only be made by wood smoke from cooking fires in houses. Plainview. Six, maybe eight miles. He put his gun belt over his shoulders as before, and carried the gunman's weapon in his hand. He resumed his jogging. With any luck he would be in Plainview before sunset.

When Fargo walked into town about seven that evening, he went to the sheriff's office and reported the dead man in the brush and where the corpse could be found. He turned in the man's weapon, his purse, and the letter with the name and St. Louis address.

"You're causing me all sorts of trouble here, Fargo. Now I'll have to take two men and a wagon out to bring in the body and bury it. Then notify the next of kin, if any."

"Sorry, but better him than me you're going to bury. How is Kirk Gaylord?"

"Just a shoulder wound. Doc patched him up, and he went back to his office. I saw a light in his place a few minutes ago, so he must still be there. This jasper you shot, he say anything about who paid him to gun down Kirk Gaylord?"

"Not a word. I planned on bringing him back and making him talk, but it didn't turn out that way."

The sheriff looked up and lit a cigar. "Yeah, Fargo, I know what you mean. I've been in those boots a time or two."

"You warn Kirk to be careful?"

"Did that. His brother is in town for the will reading. First I heard about a will."

"That's one of the items still missing from the registered mail. It can make a big difference for Kirk, his brother, and his sister about how much inheritance they each receive."

"No wonder there's been such a crime surge in my town. Be glad when it's over."

Fargo waved at the sheriff and headed for Kirk's office. The light still showed in his window over the hardware store. Fargo climbed the steps and pushed open the door.

Kirk trained a shotgun on Fargo's chest.

Fargo walked in and nodded. "Yes, good move, but not good enough. That's a single shot. After your first shot kills the man at the door, the second man steps up and puts five slugs into your heart."

"What do you mean, second man?"

"If they hire one, they could hire three or four. How much is that hide of yours worth stretched out in a casket?"

"Under the old will, one point three million dollars. Under the new one, about three million. I see what you mean." Fargo locked the door, then slid a wooden chair under the knob so it couldn't be opened without breaking the chair.

"Now, stay away from the windows. Pull blinds from the wall side. Don't make yourself an easy target."

"You chased the man who shot me?"

"I did. He didn't have time to say who hired him before he died."

"So where does that leave me? I don't have the new will. The reading is set for tomorrow."

"Postpone it. Tell the judge the robbery of the registered mail created an unforeseen problem that prevented you from getting the true will for the court to read. You should be able to talk him into a week's delay."

"I'll try it."

"In the meantime, keep yourself alive. You have a bodyguard? A man who can shoot who will protect you?"

"No." He scowled. "But looks like I better get one. I didn't think my brother would stoop so low as to pay somebody to kill me, just so he could get more of the inheritance."

Fargo left and went toward the hotel. On the way he passed the newspaper office. The lights were still on. He tried the door, unlocked. Fargo stepped inside and looked around, but couldn't see anyone. He went through a curtain into the back where he spotted Sarah Wellford standing at a type case. She wore blue bib overalls and an ink-smudged blue blouse.

He called out a hello, and she jumped. When he walked over, she put down a long, thin metal tray and punched him in the shoulder.

"If I had pied that stick of type I just spent an hour setting, I'd have clobbered you with a monkey wrench." She brushed blonde hair back from her face and left a smudge of oil on her cheek. "So, what do you think of my back shop work clothes?"

"Practical, almost as dirty as mine."

"Did you catch him?"

"Who?"

"The bushwhacker who back-shot Kirk Gaylord, who you rode out after this afternoon?"

"Woman, do you know everything that goes on in this town?"

"No, but the things I don't know, I'm working on." She grinned and smudged her other cheek moving back some errant blonde locks. "It's my break time. Would you like some home-brewed coffee?"

"Only if you grind the beans."

She smiled brightly and led the way to the side of the building, where a small table had been set up near a cook stove. A fire in the box had heated the coffee on top. She checked the pot.

"Sometimes it's strong, sometimes weak. You take your chances."

They both stood beside the table. "Hand me those cups," she said. He reached for them and leaned close to her. He stopped and then pushed in closer and angled his lips down to hers. She didn't move. The kiss was soft and gentle, and when he broke away, her eyes stayed closed for a moment longer.

"Nice," she said. "But I can do better." She turned toward him, caught his neck, pulled down his head, and kissed him hard and firm, holding it while pushing her breasts against his buckskin shirt. She clung to him a moment, then let go.

"Better," he said. He grinned and watched her. "But . . ."

She laughed. "But you can do better? Show me."

This time his arms went around her, and he crushed her slender body hard against his. His mouth opened and his tongue drove at her lips until they parted and let him explore her mouth. As they settled together, she whimpered softly until he eased back from her.

She watched him coyly. "Mr. Fargo, would you like to come to my house, where I can serve you some hot cherry pie with fresh whipped cream, and some of my better coffee?"

He nodded. "Be delighted. But only if I can wash up first."

"Done," she said. She unbuckled the shoulder straps on her overalls and slipped them off. He saw she had on a pair of men's pants. She giggled at his reaction.

"I'm doing a man's work here. Least I can do is dress like a man, so I don't get grease and ink all over my dresses."

Ten minutes later, they had closed up the newspaper office, and walked a block and a half to a small cottage down from Main Street. It had a white picket fence around a yard with grass and bordered by what she told him were wildflowers.

"I love to collect wildflowers and save the seed. Then I plant it here in the spring. I have mint, golden rod, asters, wild milkweed, and verbena. You should see them in the daylight when they're all in bloom."

Inside he found a well-furnished cottage, with a living room, a kitchen, two bedrooms, and a sink in the kitchen with a pitcher pump attached.

"Water right in the kitchen," he marveled.

"We're getting modern and sophisticated here in Plainview."

"Bet you don't have a bathtub," he said.

She chuckled. "So you want me to give you a bath?"

"Been known to happen. But then I'd need to give you a bath, too."

"Let's settle for washing hands and faces, for now," she said.

They washed up and dried on fluffy towels. Then he tilted her head back and kissed her long and deep.

"I really don't want any cherry pie after all," she said softly when the kiss ended.

He picked her up and carried her to a closed door off the living room. The bedroom was small with a single bed and a real mattress set high on springs. He put her down on the bedspread on her back and let her blonde hair flow over the pillow, then bent down and kissed her. He lit a lamp and set it on the dresser. Then he pushed the curtains closed on the bedroom window.

She frowned. "I don't want you to think—"

"I don't," he said, and kissed her again. Then he unbuttoned her smudged blue blouse. When he pushed it back on both sides, he found a chemise under it. Fargo sat her up and took the blouse off her arms, then lifted the chemise over her head. Her breasts angled toward him and bounced and swayed in the soft lamplight.

"Beautiful," he said. "So perfect, just magnificent." He reached out and touched one breast. She gave a little sigh as both his hands found her luscious orbs and he massaged them gently. He ran his finger around the large pink areolas, then tweaked her nipples until she moaned softly.

"So good . . . oh yes, that feels so wonderful." He kissed her again, and this time her tongue drove into his mouth and fervently explored. He lifted her breasts, pushed them together, and kneaded them both again.

He bent down and licked her breasts, going around and

around until he came to the top, and there he nibbled at her nipples with his teeth.

"Oh God, oh God, but that feels incredible."

She pushed her hands down to his crotch and explored. He opened the buttons on the fly and let her hands creep inside. Quickly she worked through his underpants and found his manhood stiff and sturdy already.

Sarah's eyes glowed. "Oh, he's so . . . so strong. So huge."

As he worked a series of kisses around her soft belly, Sarah lifted her hips off the bed so he could pull down her pants, taking them off her feet. Now she wore only bloomers. They were made of soft cotton, tight at the waist with a short skirt and loose trousers gathered at the knee.

Fargo stared at the underclothes in wonder.

"They're the latest thing from New York," Sarah said. "Yes, silly, they come off easy." She pushed down the tops, then he helped and pulled them off her legs.

He marveled at her tiny waist, her flaring hips supported by slender, curvaceous legs, and a blonde thatch at her crotch. She wasn't shy about being naked in front of him. Instead she sat up and tugged at the buttons on his buckskin shirt until he pulled it off. She rubbed his black chest hair and then worked at his pants until he stood and dropped them. Soon he stood in front of her as naked as she was. She surged off the bed and stood facing him, then pushed her hips against his, pressed her breasts hard into his chest, and nestled her head on his shoulder. Fargo was excited by her aggressiveness.

"You don't know how often I dream of doing this with a handsome, well-built man like you. I'm overwhelmed that you're here. Any way I can please you will be my joy." She knelt in front of him and stroked his iron rod, moving her hand up and down slowly, then faster. Then before he could do more than gasp, she bent and took him in her mouth. She bounced on him a dozen times, and then he pushed her away.

"Too soon," he said. "Later." He lifted her onto the bed on her back, and his hands went to her legs, caressing up one almost to her crotch, then back down. Her legs spread and she mewled softly. She caught one hand and pushed it far down, where his fingers brushed across her moist center, and she wailed in delight.

"Again, do that again," she whispered. He did, and she caught his hand and moved one finger over her round, hard clit. Then she spread her legs more and began a soft little motion with her hips as he strummed her like a guitar.

Sarah suddenly erupted with a wail, and her hips pounded hard upward against his hand as she bucked upward again and again. He waited for her to boil over and simmer down. Soon she gasped and shuddered and opened her eyes.

"Marvelous. So wonderful." She caught his manhood and pumped it back and forth a dozen times before he took her hand away.

"Right now, darling Fargo. Right now deep and hard and hot and long. Poke it into me, right now."

He knelt between her spread legs and lifted her knees. He felt for her honey pot, found it and spread the juices, then surged forward.

Sarah shrieked when he entered her, then she cried. He stopped and she shook her head.

"Go, go, I love it. Tears of joy." She kept crying in ecstasy as he drove forward and her hips bounced up to meet him. Then it was a race to see who could outlast the other.

Sweat beaded on Fargo's forehead as he pounded away, and she matched him stroke for stroke. At last he could hold it no longer and he exploded, shredding himself into a million pieces that shot into the sky. Then he felt as if he began to sink through the sky with the weight of his gathered body until he landed softly on the bed in a small white-fenced cottage in Plainview.

Sarah had cried through it all, erupting with a series of wild wails as she climaxed and then went limp, her eyes closed. For a few seconds she stopped breathing. When he frowned at her condition, she opened her eyes and chuckled softly.

"Fooled you," she said. Then they both laughed and clung to each other as their breath came in ragged gasps and surges until they could breathe normally again.

At last Fargo moved off and lay beside her, his arm under her head, pulling her to his shoulder.

She looked up at him. "I want you to stay here tonight. Isn't this better than some old hotel room?"

"Do you cook breakfast?"

"The best. Waffles and bacon and eggs and toast and jam and coffee made with real beans that I ground myself."

"Might talk me into it."

"I'll try." She grinned. "I'll try again later on when you get your strength back. How about an hour?"

"Twenty minutes," he whispered, and they both laughed.

The next morning, on Skye's way to the sheriff's office the postmistress, Mrs. Olson, stopped him outside the post office.

"Some small boy turned in this Bible. He said maybe I could recognize some of the names in it. I don't. I thought maybe it was part of the missing mail."

"There was a missing Bible," Fargo said. "I'll take it to the sheriff since the postal inspector is gone. Thanks."

The sheriff looked over the Bible and tried to decipher the names written in the flyleaf. At last on the bottom of the last page he found the name of Sadie Utley. "That's the name of the woman who had a Bible missing," the sheriff said.

Fargo said it was. He looked at it but could find no thousand-dollar bills in it. There was evidence something sticky might have been on the back cover.

"Leave it here, I'll get it back to Mrs. Utley," the sheriff said.

Fargo checked in at the bank. The manager said two more of the stolen bills had come in, but the merchants couldn't remember who had spent them. More dead ends. While he was in the bank, Mr. Delano came in. He wanted to talk to the manager. After they had talked a minute, the manager waved Fargo over to his desk.

"Mr. Delano, tell Fargo what you told me," the manager said.

Delano looked up and nodded. "Got this message writ on tablet paper that said I could get my bearer bonds back by bringing a thousand dollars to a certain place. We'd make the exchange and I'd still have four thousand dollars."

"Mr. Delano, it sounds like a swindle or a trap," Fargo said. "Whoever wrote this note doesn't understand how bearer bonds work. If he has them, he could cash them just like a check. They are like cash."

"But what if he really does have my bonds?" Mr. Delano asked.

Fargo shook his head. "It's almost a hundred percent chance that the person who wrote this is simply trying to swindle the money from you."

The manager cleared his throat and motioned to Fargo to come to one side.

"I'm sure you're right, but it might help put the old guy's mind at ease if you went to the meet. What could it hurt?"

Fargo nodded. Back at the desk he looked at the old man.

"When and where are you supposed to take the money? I'll do it for you, only I won't have real money, just cut-up paper in a satchel."

Ephraim Delano blinked back grateful tears as he gave Fargo a hug. Then he told him where and when the exchange was to take place.

An hour later, Fargo rode the Ovaro a mile out of town to a bend in the river where a huge oak tree had once been used for hanging. He had a small leather case on his saddle filled with cut-up paper the size of dollar bills. On the outside of one bundle he had two one-dollar bills and another on the back. From a distance the stack would look real enough. The meet was set for eleven o'clock. Fargo got there a half hour early and checked the obvious bush-whacking positions. None were good. He picked out one and waited.

Promptly at eleven a rider came fast from the town road. He reined up at the oak and looked around.

"Hey, old man, if you're hiding, you can see I don't have a weapon, not even a six-gun. I do have the bonds, though. Come on out and show me the money and I'll give them to you."

Fargo rode out fast on the Ovaro. The rider on the bay looked nervous but held his position. He held up a large paper envelope over a foot square.

"Got them right here," the man said.

Fargo had never seen him before. Fargo held up one of the bundles of bills with the real money on the outside. "I've got the cash."

They rode closer together. Fargo watched the other man for nervousness and soon saw it all over. He was sweating, and his hand shook as he held the envelope. He pushed his feet in and out of the stirrups.

Fargo drew the Colt and fired a round over the swindler's head. "Drop the envelope right there and see how fast you can ride toward St. Louis," Fargo commanded.

The young man started to reach in his jacket for what Fargo figured was a hideout. Fargo fired again, knocking the high crowned hat off the man's head. "The envelope now, or the next one goes into your knee and you'll never walk again without a limp."

"Bastard."

"Some call me worse. Drop it or I'm firing in three seconds. One, two . . ." The man dropped the envelope and spurred the horse away from Plainview. Fargo stepped down from his pinto and retrieved the envelope. It had nothing in it but some pieces of cut-up cardboard.

Back in town, Fargo showed the envelope to Mr. Delano. His shoulders slumped and he sat down in the bank's one lobby chair. "Don't know what I'm gonna do. Daughter wants me to come to Denver. Way out there in the wilderness. Ain't even a train there."

The bank manager brought him a cup of coffee. "Mr. Delano, you promised me you'd give the railroad a week to find your bonds. We have four more days."

Fargo headed for the courthouse. He had promised Kirk Gaylord that he would be there for the reading of the will. Fargo would testify about the lost mail if he had to. He wasn't fond of courts and judges, but he had to do this for the wounded businessman. Fargo walked up to the courthouse and opened the door.

8

Judge Weatherly Bartholomew had arrived in Plainview the evening before after traveling two days by stage and train from western Missouri. He was still tired, grumpy, and had spent all morning and afternoon settling petty disputes that should have been taken care between neighbors without involving his court.

Now he looked down from his raised bench at three siblings bickering over a will. He admitted to the group that it was a substantial sum, slightly over three million dollars, according to all parties. He had sat through pleadings by both sides, and had ordered the participants and lawyers to sit down and be quiet.

The will stipulated that it be read in a court of law to make it binding. One brother's lawyer, Ormly Quant from St. Louis, asked that the reading be postponed due to the theft of important registered mail that contained the latest and true will of the deceased. He asked for a week to find the true will.

Judge Bartholomew blew his nose. It never seemed to stop dripping. He'd have to go back to snorting salt water the way his doctor told him. What would a week matter? He looked up from bloodshot eyes.

"Once more a simple statement of your pleadings. I don't want to hear from lawyers. I want to hear the brothers. Mr. Kirk Gaylord. You're first."

"Your Honor, the theft of registered mail two days ago has temporarily denied us the ability to present the only legal copy of the new will that our father wrote and signed two months before his death. It is imperative that we have that will to present to Your Honor."

"Mmmmm. Yes. Now, Mr. Terrance Gaylord."

"Your Honor, we have in hand the last legal will and testament of my father, dated a year and a half ago. I have seen no new will. I and my sister don't think such a will was ever written and does not exist. This is a devious delaying tactic by my brother to try to cheat my sister and I out of our third of our late father's estate."

Judge Bartholomew waved Terrance back to his chair. He coughed and spat into his ready handkerchief. Damn, more flecks of blood. He'd have to tell his doctor about that. He coughed once more and then looked at the six people in the court.

"Mr. Kirk Gaylord. I haven't heard any evidence that there indeed was a theft of registered mail. Can you present any witness who can bear that out?"

"I can, Your Honor. I call Skye Fargo."

Fargo stood and walked to the witness stand and was sworn in.

"Young man, is that dress proper for a courtroom?"

"Your Honor, for nearly a hundred years of our young nation's existence, buckskins were worn not only by the population, but under the robes of our magistrates and judges as well."

"Yes. Do you know about the robbery?"

"I do, Your Honor. I am an investigator for the railroad. I tracked the robbers from the train, found a campsite where the train robbers were killed and buried by two unknown riders. A short distance on, I found two sacks of registered mail, torn up and scattered over a considerable area. I recovered the pieces of the mail and returned all of it to a U.S. postal inspector here in Plainview two days ago."

"Any questions?" the judge asked, looking at Terrance's lawyer, a local man named Hirum Shaw.

"Yes, Your Honor. Mr. Fargo. Did you find a will in the torn up registered mail?"

"No, but there was—"

"That's all. No more questions."

The judge scowled. "I'd like to hear the rest of the witness's testimony. Please continue."

"No will was found there, but when the inspectors checked all of the records, they found that a registered piece had been sent to Kirk Gaylord from St. Louis. It was one of six pieces of mail missing."

"But you don't know that the missing registered item sent to Kirk Gaylord was a will, do you, Mr. Fargo?" Shaw asked.

"No."

"Enough," the judge said. "To allow for fair action here, I'm postponing this hearing for a week so that proper discovery can be carried out. If the will is found in that time, I'm stipulating that it may be read under the jurisdiction of this court with Judson Jerome, counsel of this town, as the presiding judge in my absence. This hearing is closed."

Outside the courthouse, Kirk shook his lawyer's hand.

"You did it, Ormley, you did it. Now we have to find that will. Who could have stolen it besides my brother?"

"We don't have any evidence that Terrance stole the will."

"True, but who else would do it? Nobody else would have benefited."

"At least we have a week to find it," Quant said.

Three weeks ago, Sarah Wellford had met a young woman in Sally's Millinery shop. They both were looking at the same perky little hat. Both tried it on and both liked it. Sarah said she could wait for a new hat and let the other woman buy it. Sarah liked her and asked her to go to the café for coffee.

"Oh, I'm sorry, but I can't do that. I'm not supposed to. I

mean, my manager doesn't even want me to come out to this shop, but I come in the back door."

Sarah was stunned. "Why, for goodness sakes? I don't understand."

The woman was nineteen, pretty, slender, almost too thin. Her smile was glorious and her hair long and coppery red. She stared at Sarah for a moment. "You really don't know, do you? I'm Kelly. I work at the Whisper Saloon. I'm a fancy lady."

Sarah's eyes went wide, and she grabbed Kelly's hand. "But you're so pretty, so nice."

Kelly's grim smile couldn't hide her shame. "Sure, I'm pretty and nice, and that means I'm worth two dollars for a half hour. I'm sorry I shocked you. You buy the hat. I don't have anywhere to wear it anyway." Kelly turned and hurried out the back door to the alley that led to the rear entrance to the Whisper Saloon.

Sarah turned to Sally, who owned the store.

"Now, you know," Sally said, "Kelly must like you. She doesn't even talk to anyone when she's in here. I like her, poor thing. I don't know how I can help her, though. I wonder if she's good with a needle and thread?"

"I want to talk to her again," Sarah said. "Maybe I can do a story on her about what a hard life it is for the girls. Didn't we have a fancy lady commit suicide just last month?"

"Happens more than we know. Doc Andrews tells me it's happened five times this past year. He covers them up. They have nothing to look forward to."

Sarah had arranged for Sally to send someone to get her the next time Kelly came into her shop. After two weeks they had met three times in the shop, and at last Kelly had agreed to let Sarah interview her for a story, as long as her real or fancy names weren't used.

Sarah had arranged for Kelly to come to the back door of the newspaper office today for a second interview. She promised to bring some of the weird things customers left behind. Kelly came right on time with a filled cardboard box.

Sarah had a long list of questions. She made coffee and had a tray of sweet rolls on the table at the side of the back shop. The interview went well, and Kelly told Sarah everything she wanted to know. She found out where Kelly came from, how she had been forced into prostitution when a neighbor boy got her pregnant and wouldn't marry her. Her Methodist parents threw her out of the house without any money, not even a bag full of her clothes. Kelly had supported herself the only way she knew how.

"Look at some of the things the guys leave behind," Kelly said. She showed Sarah a left boot, a gold pocket watch, three town hats, a set of garters, three envelopes with papers in them, a compass, a wooden leg, a man's wig, four fountain pens, six combs, and a dozen handkerchiefs. "Most of it I just throw away, but first I keep it for a year or so in case somebody comes hunting something."

The interview went on for another hour, and Sarah figured she had enough for a good story.

"I promise I won't identify you in any way, Kelly. That will be our secret. Not even your madam will know. I just wish there was something I could do to help you."

Kelly sighed. "I've tried to figure how I could break out of there a dozen times. Josie is supposed to be saving our money for us, but who knows if she is. I should have almost a hundred dollars, but I doubt if I'll ever see it."

"Kelly, if you want to break away, you let me know and I'll march right in there and wring your money out of Josie. She's not that tough."

They stood and Sarah hugged Kelly, then let her out the back door to the alley. Sarah frowned. She was going to have to do something to help that girl. She couldn't work at the paper, since she could barely read. Her parents never let her go to school much because they traveled around. Sarah knew she had to think of something.

Fargo took a cold beer from the apron at the Round-house bar, hoping he'd get some word about Dutch. Nobody seemed to know the man. Fargo sat there drinking beer, cooling off under a slow-moving fan. Judy, the fancy lady he'd talked to before, flounced up and sat in the chair across from him.

They said hi and she turned serious. "Weird thing happened to me last night just after supper. Some young kid, maybe fourteen, slipped in the back door and up the stairs to my room. I was taking a little rest when he popped in. He dropped his pants and showed me a roll of twenty-dollar bills. Said he'd give me a hundred dollars for a quick poking."

"Young kid? Did he have pimples all over his face?"

Judy snorted. "How the hell could you know that? He sure did. Looked terrible. He had a boner on and threw the hundred dollars at me. I threw it back at him, and kicked him out of my room, and threw his pants after him."

"You turned down a hundred dollars?"

"Yeah, you bet. If Sheriff Crosby heard I'd done a kid like that, he'd ridden me out of town on a flat car spread-eagled and naked. He don't tolerate no kid poking. Least-wise, I haven't heard from the kid again. Them bills he showed me was plain new. Fact is, he didn't get all of them. I kept one as a souvenir." She held out a new twenty without a wrinkle or a fold. "I heard about the stolen money."

Fargo checked the serial number. "Yeah, that's one of the bills from the railroad robbery. How in hell did this kid get his hands on the new bills?"

"Guess he didn't do the robbery."

"Nope, them two gents who did had an early funeral for their trouble. You know this kid? Seen him around town?"

"I don't see many kids in my line of work."

"Yeah, true. He's been spending those twenties all over town. By now I have half the merchants watching for him. By the way, I have to keep the twenty and turn it in. Stolen money can't be spent."

"I figured. Otherwise, I would have kept it for a year or so. Hey, handsome, you have time for a quick one?"

"I'd like to, but my beer is about gone, and I'm supposed to be working."

"I'd give you a workout."

Fargo grinned. "I just bet you would. Maybe later."

He finished the beer and went out to the street. Lewis, one of the deputy sheriffs, found Fargo a half block up the boardwalk.

"Sheriff's looking for you, Mr. Fargo. He says to come right down to the jail."

At the sheriff's office, four men were checking rifles and shotguns, getting ready. Sheriff Crosby looked up.

"Fargo, I figured you'd want to be in on this. Got a telegram from a St. Louis bank that a deposit made today by mail contained $500 of that bank robbery money. He said every bank in the country has those serial numbers."

"So who made the deposit?"

"J. Logan of 12 Elm Street, Plainview. Looks like we might have a break on that train robbery."

There were five of them in the raid. Fargo took a sheriff's rifle and stood across the street beside a house where the sheriff positioned him. They had one man covering each corner of the house. The sheriff checked to be sure everyone was in place, then he walked up and knocked on the door at 12 Elm. He waited, then knocked again.

At last the door edged open. The sheriff couldn't see into the dark room.

"I'm Sheriff Crosby. Is there a J. Logan here?"

The door came fully open, revealing a frail little woman in a bathrobe. She had pure white hair and wrinkles on her wrinkles. She was at least eighty years old.

"I'm Jocelyn Logan. What can I help you with, Sheriff?"

Sheriff Crosby eased off on the six-gun he had behind his back. "You the only J. Logan here?"

"Only one who's been here the last five years. Is there some trouble?"

"Did you mail some cash money to a St. Louis bank to make a deposit opening a new account?"

"Certainly not, young man. I do my banking here in town, what precious little there is of it."

"You didn't send five hundred dollars in cash by mail to St. Louis day before yesterday?"

"Sheriff, I haven't seen five hundred dollars cash money since my late husband died back in forty-eight. Now, if you don't mind, I have work to do. My great-grandchildren are coming for supper, and I'm not near ready for them. Anything else?"

"Afraid that we've made a mistake, Mrs. Logan. Good afternoon."

A block away in a two-story hotel, two men with field glasses stood at a rear window and watched the sheriff's raid on the Logan house. The room was dark so no one could look into it, and the men could watch without being seen. One of the men was large, solid, and smoked a cigar. He wore a gold chain across his vest pockets with a gold nugget in the center.

The second man was Dutch, wearing his bowler hat. Dutch swore. "Well, you were right. No chance we can deposit any of the money in any bank. They must have sent the numbers to every bank in the country. Just beats me up that I'll soon have over seven thousand dollars, and I won't be able to spend a cent of it."

The large man nodded. "This was a good test. It was only five hundred dollars. It was a lesson well learned. Now we'll look for some other way to cleanse the money so we can use it."

Dutch slammed his hand against the wall. "Why is it so damned complicated? It looked easy when we planned it all out. Now it's turned into a nest of rattlesnakes. I still say I should eliminate this Trailsman."

"No, that would bring federal marshals into it, and they are not a good bunch to have chasing you. After another two or three days it should begin to wind down. We lay low and we have no real problems. There is no way they can tie either of us to the robbery or the missing money. Just relax and think how much fun you're going to have with all that money when you move to New York City."

On the walk back to the sheriff's office, Fargo told the lawman about the pimple-faced kid. "He tried to con a fancy lady into doing him last night. Offered her a hundred dollars, and she kept one twenty before she booted him out." Fargo handed the bill to the Sheriff. "It's one of the stolen bills."

"Don't know why we can't find him," the sheriff said. "Not many kids his age around here. We haven't seen hide nor skedaddle of him anywhere in town. Just have to look harder."

As he walked away from the sheriff, Fargo tried to put the pieces together. A train robbed, three men killed, perhaps a fourth murder connected with the robbery. Were the killings done to make a trail harder to follow? Were the culprits here in town? The men who had killed the actual train robbers probably brought the loot here to town, then could have left on the train. Some of the money was still here. He had hard evidence of that with the twenty-dollar bills that had turned up. Who was spending them?

Surely the men with the loot would know better than to spend it here in town. Was the missing will a part of the whole scheme? Or was it just an unhappy coincidence for Kirk Gaylord? Maybe the robbery was aimed at the will, and the cash and gold in the safe were bonuses. Then there was Terrance Gaylord, the brother who stood to lose eight hundred thousand dollars. How did he figure in? Could he be behind a conspiracy to rob the mail to get the will that would cost him a huge chunk of his father's estate?

Then the two men in the alley the old drunk heard arguing. Dutch was the name the drunk heard. Was he part of it? It certainly sounded like it, if Fargo could believe a rummy who was a former cop.

Dutch had to be his best key. Fargo haunted the saloons again, and at last, at the lowest-class drinking and whoring spot in town, Fargo finally found a man who would talk.

Chris Balker lifted the new mug of beer to salute Fargo, who had just bought it for him.

"Oh, yeah, I know Dutch. Dutch Pendleton. He's a skunk, a sidewinder, a back stabber. The bastard almost killed me about a year ago. Loves his knife. Never carries a gun, but he always has at least three knives. One he wears under his long-sleeve shirt. He can flick his wrist and the blade pops out, four inches of the sharp steel. He's real good with it.

"Hell, I was drunk and didn't know who he was. He bumped into me and I threw my beer in his face and he came at me with the blade without saying a word. He cut me six times before I hit him with a chair and knocked him out. Guys watching me told me to take his knife and slit his throat. I should have. Lord knows, I should have."

"He's back in town?"

"True blue. I'll even tell you where he lives. I make it a point not to go anywhere he does. He probably doesn't remember me. I grew a beard since then, but I still don't take chances."

"Where does he live?"

"Ma Scudder's boardinghouse, a block in back of the train station. Can't miss it. Sits on the corner of Ash and Alder."

"Thanks. Could you use a couple more beers?"

"Lord almighty, I certainly can."

Fargo flipped him a silver dollar. Chris caught it in the

air. If he didn't lose his change, the dollar would buy him twenty more beers.

"One more thing, Chris. Can you describe him for me? What does he look like? What does he wear?"

"Easy. He's maybe five-eight, slender as a toothpick. Wears a brown suit most of the time with a black bowler. Stands out in a crowd. A natty dresser. White shirt, stiff collar, and a tie. A real fashion plate."

"Thanks." Fargo left and checked the saloons again. He moved just inside the door in the usually dark drinking emporiums and scanned the trade without letting most of the patrons notice him. He knew his buckskins made him stand out. He found his man in the second best saloon in town, the Bloody Bucket. It wasn't the fanciest, but the men said it had the best whores in town.

Fargo pulled back and went across the street, leaned a chair back against the railroad station wall, and watched the door of the Bloody Bucket. His man didn't come out until just after five that afternoon. Dutch went directly to the Farm Home Café. Fargo strolled in five minutes later and took a seat at a table at the far end of the place where he could watch Dutch, who had taken off the black bowler when he sat down.

Fargo had pot roast stew with six different vegetables mixed in the gravy. For dessert there was cherry pie and whipped cream. He'd been thinking about that ever since Sarah mentioned it last night. He finished his meal before Dutch did, paid, and left. He took a position down the street and waited.

Dutch came out ten minutes later, looked around, then headed down the boardwalk. He turned into the alley and went in the side door of the Hallmark Hotel, the best one in town. It was not a good idea to follow him in there. Dutch didn't live there, so why would he go there after dark?

Fargo moved to a new spot where he could see the side and front doors of the hotel and not be obvious. Five minutes later, a man Fargo knew was Terrance Gaylord went to the front door, and walked inside like he belonged there.

A half hour of waiting produced no more traffic for the side entrance to the hotel. It made Fargo wonder if the two were meeting secretly in the hotel. If so, why?

On the way to his hotel room, Fargo walked past the train station and saw a light on in the district manager's office. The Trailsman realized he hadn't made a report to him for over a day, and figured this was a good time.

Neville looked up the moment Fargo came in. He laid down the pen he was writing with and leaned back in the big chair.

"Fargo. Wondered what you've been doing. Any closer to nailing down these outlaws who have made the Missouri & Illinois Central look so bad? I've got the vice president sending me two telegrams a day asking for progress. Just what the hell is happening?"

"Not a lot, Mr. Neville. I told you we found that one bill from the stolen money. Some drifter evidently spent it in a saloon and left the next morning on the train. We found the missing Bible, but not much else of the stolen mail. The sheriff and I are working on it. We hope to have something soon."

"I've been told to cut off your employment. In three days your second week will be over, and that's the end of the ride. You'll be paid for the two weeks, but not the third we had originally talked about. We had no contract, just talk about how long we might need you. Agreed?"

"Even if I haven't found the conspirators in this robbery?"

"That's what the vice president told me. Out of my hands. Sorry."

"I'll get back to work and hope to have it wrapped up within the next three days."

"Do that." Neville puffed on his cigar and tried to blow a smoke ring over his desk. It formed only a lazy half circle.

Fargo walked out of the office and into the soft Missouri summer evening. He decided to check back at the Hallmark Hotel. Terrance was from out of town. It was reasonable that he could have rented a room at the hotel. But not Dutch. He went in the front door and rang the bell on the desk for the clerk to come. He stepped out of a back room.

"Evening, need a room?"

"Looking for Terrance Gaylord. Does he have a room here?"

"Why, yes, he came in yesterday. Said he'll be staying on for a few more days. Something about reading his father's will."

"He asked me to meet him here. What's his room number?"

"He's in two-oh-six on the second floor."

"I was supposed to meet Dutch Pendleton here. Do you know if he's arrived?"

"Fact is, he came about a half hour ago. Went right up to Mr. Gaylord's room. Second floor."

"Thanks, I'll find it." He went up the steps to the second floor, down to the back stairway, and out into the alley. So, that was the real news. Terrance Gaylord was meeting with Dutch Pendleton, who just might be involved in some way with the train robbery.

Fargo headed for his hotel. On the way he passed the newspaper office and saw the lights on. He tried the door; it was open, so he went in.

Sarah looked up from where she was working at her desk at the left side of the office. She smiled and waved.

"Come on in, I'm running late. I need a break. How would you like to go to dinner with a lady if she picked up the check?"

"Not a chance on the check, and I just had dinner. But I'll have some coffee and watch you eat."

"Have I got a good story to tell you. It won't be in this issue but certainly the next one. I'm still writing your story about the railroad robbery."

"Can I see an advance proof?"

"Not a chance. You'll have to wait for it like everyone else. All I need is an ending. How close are you to solving the robbery?"

"Probably not close enough for this issue."

9

Nate Frazer had waited on the train when it pulled into Plainview until everyone else had left, and just before it headed on west. He poked his head out of the passenger car, and when he was sure that no one was watching for him, he stepped off the train and moved as quickly as he could without running into the station. He paused again, checked out the people in the terminal, and when he saw no one was interested in him, he walked across the street. Frazer slipped down the boardwalk and into a saloon where no one knew him. He had to retrace his steps of two nights before. The big man had given him the package and the hundred dollars and told him to be sure to be on that train.

He'd promised that night that he would and it had been easy. He'd been so keyed up about making a hundred here and another hundred in St. Louis that he couldn't even piss straight. He decided a small celebration was in order, so he bought a bottle and played solitaire for three hands, and lost all of them. He looked at the poker games, but knew he wasn't good at poker. How long did he stay in this saloon that fatal night? Or was this the saloon he went to after he talked to the big man with the money? He did know that it was in the second saloon where he found the right girl. Yeah, he'd looked here, but the whores were not at all what he wanted. He needed somebody less brassy, low-key, even a little shy. Not easy to find those qualities in a fancy lady. Usually it had to be somebody relatively new to the business, who hadn't been ground down by the hard life that these women led.

But he had found the right one in the second saloon, he remembered that for sure. The only trouble was, he couldn't remember the name of the next saloon he went to. He tried and tried, but still he couldn't remember. Had he dumped the package when he was drinking, or in the whore's room, or afterward when he walked down the street to a new saloon? Dammit, he couldn't tie it down. Had he had the package when he left the first saloon?

Yes. He had it, because he hadn't emptied the bottle he bought, and he remembered having to juggle the bottle and the package. He had done that all the way to the second drinking emporium.

Frazer went out and walked down the street, trying to figure out exactly where he had gone next. He knew by this time that Dutch would know that he hadn't delivered the package in St. Louis. The damn telegraph would get word to Dutch quickly. The question was, would Dutch look for him right here in town? That would be a dumb thing to do after he messed up with that will worth over three million dollars. So why was he here? He had to know where he left the thing. Get it back, give it to Dutch. He just hoped it didn't get him killed. There was a hell of a lot of money involved here. He went in the other two saloons, but they just didn't seem right.

He remembered a piano. Had it been playing in the cathouse or somewhere else? Yeah, the girls kind of danced down the stairs to start the night's work, he recalled. But which one was that?

Frazer turned and walked down the street to the Round-house Saloon. He figured they would have a piano there and maybe a girl singer. He was right. The big upright piano with half the white ivory keys missing stood near a little stand where the girl would sing. She wasn't there yet. But was this the spot where he had met the young girl he had pleasured with? He had a beer and looked around.

About half the girls were sitting at the tables and a few working men at the bar. None of them looked young enough to have caught his eye that night.

A few minutes later, he checked out each of the girls waiting for business. Then he was positive none of them was the right one. Maybe he'd check back later, when all of the girls were on duty.

Reluctantly, he went on to look over the Bucket of Blood. The second best spot in town for a good whore. Maybe she was there. He was two stores from the saloon when something sharp pricked him in the middle of the back.

"What the hell?" he blurted, and started to turn. A hand grabbed his head from behind. "Don't look back here, Frazer. Just walk straight ahead to the alley and turn in, and maybe this knife won't sever your spinal cord and put you down and dead in twenty seconds."

"Dutch?"

"You figured maybe the tooth fairy? Just keep moving. We've got some talking to do."

"Dutch, I didn't lose it on purpose. Swear to God. I didn't sell it or throw it away, I just got drunk and lost it sometime before the damned train left. I don't know where, Dutch. I'm looking for it."

Dutch pushed Frazer into the alley forcing him down until it was shadowy dark. Dutch rammed Frazer against the building and drew a thin blood line down his right cheek with a knife.

"Oh, damn, that hurts. Dutch, what the hell you doing?"

"It's been proven that a little blood helps the memory. Shall we try for another lesson?"

"I told you, dammit. Went to one saloon and got drunk. Hell, I ain't never had a hundred dollars before in my whole life. A whole fucking hundred dollars! So I bought a bottle at the Bucket of Blood and got stinking soused. Then I went to another saloon looking for my kind of whore. Hard to find. New to the business, maybe a little shy . . ."

Dutch cut a slice down Frazer's other cheek, and he screeched in pain and anger.

"Now, why you do that? I'm telling you what I did. Best I can remember."

"I'm just giving you some motivation to finish the story."

"Christ, you got a strange way of doing it. So, I went looking for my kind of whore. Don't remember if I found her or who she was or where she worked. So I'm fucked."

"Also extremely dead when the boss hears about this. You cost us each twenty-five thousand dollars. If you think I'm a little upset, you should see him. He asked me what the record was for shooting a man so many times before he died. Near as I can remember, it's forty-two. He suggests he and I try to break the record on you."

Frazer surged away from Dutch and charged down the dark alley. Dutch caught him in ten strides and tackled him around the waist. Both men rolled in the dirt and horse droppings in the alley.

"Bastard, you made me get my suit dirty. You're gonna pay to get it hand-cleaned." His blade slashed Frazer's shoulder, slicing through his shirt and making a deep cut that went all the way to the bone. Frazer screamed. Dutch slammed his hand over the wounded man's mouth, choking off the sound.

"Get up," Dutch ordered. "Then put both hands behind your back. Just so we understand each other, you try to run again, you make any little sound when we're walking, and my blade will go into your side. I'll ram it six inches through your lung and straight into your heart. You'd be dead in three minutes. Understand?"

"Yes."

"Good. We're going into the hotel side door and up to a room. You even wiggle wrong and you're dead, you got that?"

"Yes, Dutch."

A few minutes later, Dutch pushed Frazer into the room. Three lamps burned brightly. Two men were smoking cigars, and a bottle of whiskey and four glasses were set on the small table.

After Dutch told them what happened, Terrance Gaylord flew at Frazer with his fists out, and Dutch had to pull the smaller man to one side. "Hey, if anybody gets to take this poor excuse for a man apart, it's going to be me. I'll start by slicing off his toes one by one. If that don't improve his memory, I'll cut off his fingers one at a time. From there I'll do his ears next, then maybe his nose and, if he's still alive, his lying tongue." He slammed Frazer against the wall. Frazer hung there as if nailed in place. Then he began to shake. His eyes twitched and his head lolled from side to side. Then his knees began to give way, and Dutch slapped him hard in the face.

"Stand up, you fucking dead man. Stand up until I tell you to fall down."

Ormly Quant came around the table. The prisoner's eyes widened as he looked at the lawyer. There was a special glint of fury in the legal man's eyes that Dutch had never seen before.

"You lost the will? How in hell could you lose a little package like that after we paid you so well to deliver it?"

"Got drunk."

Quant drove his fist hard into Frazer's gut and doubled the man over. Dutch lifted him back to a standing position.

"Frazer, did you look inside the package?" Quant asked. "Did you know what was inside it?"

"Hell, no," Frazer gasped. "Of course not. It was confidential. All I was supposed to do was get on the six-oh-five and take it to St. Louis and deliver it to somebody."

"You were supposed to bring it to me. Instead you opened it and looked inside, didn't you?"

"No."

Quant motioned to Dutch. The small man hit Frazer twice with left jabs so fast he didn't see them coming. Then Dutch's right fist caught Frazer on the chin and jolted him sideways to the floor.

Terrance Gaylord held up his hand. "Gentlemen, just a moment. The will is lost. So it can't possibly turn up in Kirk's hands by tomorrow morning. It doesn't matter if we have it or not, just so we can be sure that Kirk doesn't have it."

"But it was lost somewhere here in town," Quant said. "Anyone might find it and turn it in to the sheriff, thinking it could be important."

"So what can we do?" Gaylord asked.

"We send Dutch out with our forgetful friend here," Quant said. "They go back over his drunken trail and turn over every stone in town until we find that damned package. Then we know for sure that when we go up in front of that lawyer playing judge tomorrow, Kirk won't magically produce the damned thing."

"Yes sir," Dutch said. "First we better tidy up those cuts on his face and shoulder." He put a handkerchief inside Frazer's shirt and held it there firmly until the bleeding stopped. Dutch swabbed down Frazer's face with whiskey to stanch the blood there. Then he jerked Frazer off the wall and shoved him toward the door. "Move it, asshole. You have a reprieve for a short time. I'll guarantee you one thing. I trusted you and you double-crossed me. That's bad for my reputation. If we don't find that damned will, I'll enjoy cutting your body into tiny pieces so nobody in the county will be able to identify you. Now let's get moving."

For two hours, Dutch and Frazer combed the town, working the saloons. At each one Dutch asked the madam of the outfit to talk to each of her girls and see if any of them remembered Frazer from two nights before and if he had left anything in their rooms. The Bucket of Blood produced no results.

They marched toward the Roundhouse Saloon. On the way, Dutch had an idea. "You get anything to eat that night? You go to one of the cafés or diners in town?"

"Don't guess I did, Dutch. Hell, I was drinking. I had my own bottle, and it warn't empty yet. On a toot like that I don't think about eating. Hell, Dutch, when you drink a lot, I bet you don't eat, either."

Dutch knew he was right.

The Roundhouse didn't turn up a thing. The madam there checked her girls, but none of them remembered Frazer that night. The last two saloons produced no clues, either.

Dutch leaned against the outside wall of the last one and stared at Frazer. "Okay, you picked up the goods, then went to the saloons. Then onto the train. You took the six-oh-five, only you didn't have the package with you, right?"

"No, I went back to the saloons and checked for the package. I didn't find it so I took the one-fifteen train for St. Louis. Figured I better get out of town before you killed me."

"You were right about that. If you didn't have it when you got on the train, you had to have lost it here in town."

"Yeah."

Dutch hunched his shoulders. He wished he could take out his knife right then, but he beat down the rage. "So where the hell is it, you sniveling bastard? What the hell did you do with it?"

Frazer put up both hands in frustration. "I don't remember. You've been drunk and didn't remember what you did sometimes. I've seen you that way myself."

Frazer dropped his hands, and Dutch chose that opening and clipped him on the jaw with his fist. Frazer's head snapped back from the force of the blow.

"We're going back to the whorehouses and check each of the sluts until we find the one you slept with. Then maybe we'll get somewhere."

Again they visited all of the whores. They even waited in the Roundhouse for the girls who were busy. When they came downstairs, none recognized Frazer and he was sure none of them were his choice. At the second saloon, a girl came down the steps from the second floor, and Frazer jumped up. "Oh, yeah, that's her. That's Kelly. I remember her now. Hey Kelly."

She walked up to them slowly, frowning when she looked at Dutch. "Hi, Nate, good to see you again."

"Hi, Kelly. Glad we found you. Hey, I'm in a little trouble. Did I leave anything in your room the other night?"

"Leave anything? Like a wallet, or a purse or a hundred-dollar bill?"

"A big envelope that had some papers in it."

"Big envelope? I've had two or three of them. I throw out all the stuff you guys leave every so often."

"We need to take a look, Kelly," Dutch said firmly.

Kelly frowned. "I don't know you. Nate can look if it's that important and he wants to."

"He wants to look right now, and I'm coming, too." Dutch herded both of them toward the stairs. Kelly started to protest, but Frazer shook his head.

"Don't get him riled up," he whispered to her.

In her room on the second floor, Kelly showed them a box that had a number of items in it. It was similar to the one she had left with Sarah at the newspaper, but another one.

"Papers, a boot, that peg leg, two pairs of eyeglasses, some bottles of pills, two pipes, three envelopes, and all sorts of other stuff."

Dutch pushed them both away and pawed through the box. He opened the envelopes and pulled out what was inside. He growled and threw the papers on the floor.

"Don't do that," Kelly snapped. "I just have to pick them up."

"Fucking whores don't talk to me like that," Dutch

barked. He turned on her, the knife snicked out from his wrist into his hand, and she backed up a step.

"Dutch, easy, take it easy. She didn't mean anything by it."

"Sure she did." He started to move up on her, but Frazer jumped in front of her.

"No, Dutch."

"Don't tell me no, you shithead!" he bellowed. He slashed with the blade, carving through Frazer's shirt, and brought a splatter of blood from his right arm.

"Come on, Dutch, the will still could be around here. Maybe I kicked it under the bed."

"Then get on your knees and look for it," Dutch yelled. Frazer looked at the smaller man a moment, then dropped to his knees and bent to look under the bed. As he did, Dutch kicked him half under the bed. A second later he jumped toward the girl. Kelly backed up to the window. She screamed.

As quick as a striking rattler, Dutch slashed with the blade at her throat. Kelly jumped sideways as the blade ripped her blouse and cut her breast, bringing a wail of pain from her. She held the wound with her hand and tried to dart around him. He waited, and when she was near enough, he drove ahead with the blade and slashed at her face, opening a long slash down her cheek. Kelly screamed again. He drew the knife back, then pushed ahead fast, jabbing the six-inch blade into her chest, above her heart.

Kelly's eyes went wide. Her hand clawed at the knife as he pulled it out. Blood coursed down her chest. She held the spot with her hand, but blood seeped around her fingers. She slid down past the window to the floor. Kelly tried to scream but found she couldn't. She tried to talk but no words came out. Her eyes opened wider, then her head tilted to one side and she slumped along the wall to the floor.

Frazer crawled out from under the edge of the bed and stood just in time to see the knife thrust and Kelly go down.

"Noooo," he bellowed, and dropped to his knees in front of her. "Easy, Kelly, easy. I'm going to get help. I'll go get the doctor. Don't move." He had started to stand when Dutch drove the six-inch blade into Frazer's back and jerked it sideways into his spinal cord. Suddenly none of Frazer's muscles did what he told them to. His head fell to his chest and he sprawled on the floor, his face smeared with Kelly's blood as his heart stopped beating.

Dutch snorted. Lifting the window, he dropped to the first floor, then scurried toward the end of the building to the back porch, jumped three feet to its roof, and then off to the ground. He was a block away before one of the girls, reacting to the screams, opened the door and found the bodies in Kelly's room.

Just before noon, Fargo sat resting in a chair with the back tipped up against the hardware store. He had been trying to figure out how Dutch and Terrance could be hooked up. The only obvious answer he could find was that Dutch was the local contact for Terrance to use to find and stop the new will from reaching Kirk Gaylord here in Plainview.

It was stretching logic a little, but he had to have something to figure with. If the two were working together, had they staged the robbery and the grabbing of the will from the registered mail? If they had it, why were they looking so worried?

He was still kicking the ideas around when a farm rig with a canvas bow-top–covered wagon came up the street, pulled by a pair of tired-looking mules. A man in blue bib overalls stepped down and tied the mules to a hitching post in front of the hardware. A farm family. The farmer motioned to the wagon. A boy about sixteen came out, followed by a girl maybe fifteen and then four more stair-step children. The smallest was about eight. A woman in a print dress and a sunbonnet came out last. The man glanced around, sent his oldest son into the hardware and then looked at the rest of the town.

Four men straggled out of the Bloody Bucket saloon. They weaved and staggered a bit and wandered toward the farm family. One of them looked hard at the blonde fifteen-year-old girl and said something to the rest of the group. They all laughed coarsely. They moved up the boardwalk and stopped in front of the family.

"Afternoon, gents," the farmer said.

"Now, ain't he neighborly," one of the drunks said.

"Nice and neighborly. Shake his hand." All four stepped into the dust of the street past the mules, and began roughly shaking hands with the farmer. Two of them went beyond him and grabbed the girl, picking her up off her feet. She shrieked.

The father turned, saw the two, and lunged at them. The other two pounded him with their fists. Slugged him half a dozen times and knocked him down, then began to kick him. One of the drunks ripped open the front of the girl's print dress, showing a white cotton chemise under it. He reached for it.

"Touch that girl again and you're a dead man."

The voice came steely soft, yet filled with anger and command. The four cowboys heard it plainly. The two cowboys with the girl looked around. The other children had scattered, and the four men stood looking at Fargo. One of the drunks snorted and reached for a six-gun in a holster on his right hip. He didn't get iron out of leather.

Fargo let the chair's front legs fall down to the boardwalk as he fired the big Colt once. The drunk going for his gun stopped and stared down at his chest, where a small hole appeared in his shirt right over his heart. He let go of the girl and slammed backward into the dust. The other three turned toward Fargo.

Two of them were in their thirties, the other one about twenty. All wore trail-stained hats and jeans. All had scraggly beards and faces that hadn't been washed for a week.

The younger man edged away from the other two.

"Lucky shot," the younger man spat.

"Want to try your luck?" Fargo asked.

"Just having a little fun."

"Didn't look like much fun for the farmer or his daughter. You boys just passing through?"

"Might be, might not be." The young man hooked his thumbs in his belt. He started to turn away, then spun back, his hand rapidly drawing iron from his holster.

From thirty feet away, Fargo shot twice. One round jolted through the man's chest. The second was centered on his forehead. The cowboy's hand didn't get the six-gun high enough to fire at Fargo, but his death reflexes made his finger pull the trigger once. The round slammed into the ground near his boots.

The farmer rose to his feet. He eyed the last two drunks. They backed up slowly until they were across the street near the railroad station. Then they turned and ran down the block. The farmer herded his family together at the far side of the wagon. His eldest son came out and stared at the two bodies lying in the dust.

Fargo stepped down into the street and checked the first man. He was dead. When he looked up, he saw Sheriff Crosby running up, his six-gun out. He looked at the corpses, then up at Fargo, then at the wagon and the huddled farm family on the far side. The sheriff pushed his range hat back on his forehead.

"Heard there was some trouble up here. Looks like I'm a little late." He looked at the crowd that had formed on the boardwalk. "Will, go get the undertaker. Tell him he has two customers."

The sheriff went through the pockets of the dead cowboys. He found identification. He took the revolvers, then went over to Fargo.

"You'll have to come down to the office and write out a

short report. Self-defense. Both them jaspers tried to draw first. The second one didn't. 'Course, he was just butt dumb to try to draw against somebody already pointing a gun. Maybe he figured you'd miss."

"Figured wrong."

The farmer came around and held out his hand to Fargo. Tears brimmed in his eyes. "I want to thank you. Don't know what I would have done. Marilyn, my oldest girl, thanks you, too. Never seen anything like this. We're new in town. Looking for a small piece of land to do some farming on. Why do men do things like that?"

"Probably because they're just naturally ill-tempered, mean, and with few principles," Fargo said. "Add to that a half dozen beers and a couple shots of whiskey, and them four probably thought they could run the whole town. My guess is, they are cattlemen looking for some work."

"Won't find any cowboy jobs around here," the sheriff said. He held out his hand to the farmer. "Name's Crosby, I'm the sheriff. Sorry about your terrible welcome to town. Usually we don't have men like that hanging around for long. My guess is that there'll be two unclaimed horses in front of the saloon over there in the morning. You're welcome to them to make up for your bad welcome from the town."

"Oh, I couldn't do that," the farmer said.

"Sure you can," Fargo said. "The sheriff will pick them out for you so there's no complaint. Those two hombres down there in the dirt aren't going to need them anymore."

The farmer looked at the two bodies. "The good Lord didn't plan on men dying that way. They have immortal souls, and right now they may be entering the gates of hell." He shook his head. "My little girl will be all right. She's strong. We don't want the horses. Sell them and pay for the cost to bury these men."

Fargo lifted his brows. The sheriff shrugged. He held out his hand again. "I didn't get your name."

"Hector Barkley, from Kentucky. Looking for some good farmland."

"Plenty of it around here, Mr. Barkley. Just take your pick. You will need to do some buying from the land office, of course."

"Much obliged, Sheriff."

"Let's get this done, Fargo. Before something else explodes around here."

As they left, the undertaker arrived with a wheelbarrow. He loaded one man in it, his feet trailing out the back and arms over the sides, and wheeled him down the street to his small office. Burial would be in the potter's field section of the cemetery tomorrow.

Fargo and the sheriff moved down the boardwalk, past the undertaker's office to the county courthouse. In the sheriff's small room, he handed Fargo a pen, ink bottle, and paper.

"Only need three or four sentences. The date, time of day, what the four staggering drunks did and said, what they did to the farmer, and what you did. Keep it short. I don't have a lot of paper."

Fargo wrote quickly, looked it over, and signed it with the date, then gave it to the sheriff.

"Good. That's the end of that. Anything new on the mail robbery or all that gold and greenbacks?"

"At least some of the cash is still here in town. That same kid spent some more, but we can't even find out who he is."

"He'll slip up sooner or later. I just hope it's before he runs out of money."

Fargo waved and left the office. He had just passed the bank and stepped up on the boardwalk on the other side of the alley when he stumbled on an uneven plank. He almost fell, twisting to his right. As he staggered forward, he felt a stinging, then a gush of pain in his left shoulder. He had been knifed. He knew the feeling; he'd been stabbed before. He jerked around. Nobody right behind him. It had to have been thrown. He didn't even bother to check his shoulder. Instead he ran to the alley, only ten feet away, and spotted a man sprinting away in the dark forty yards ahead.

Fargo took off after him, feeling the knife still in his shoulder. He realized that if he hadn't stumbled at exactly that time, the blade would be in the middle of his back and he'd be half dead lying there on the boardwalk.

10

As the man ahead rounded the corner into the street, Fargo saw that he wore a brown suit and a black bowler. Fargo rushed to the end of the alley, saw the man look over his shoulder, then dart into the back of a store.

Fargo stopped and looked at the knife in his shoulder. It wasn't a bad wound. He pulled the blade out and clamped his hand on the hole, slowing the bleeding. Then he ran again. He turned in at the same place the attacker had. It was the general store. It had a back door that led to a rear room filled with boxes and stacks of goods. A second door opened into the retail section. A store clerk stared at Fargo as he bolted into the room.

"Did a man run through here?"

"Yes," the young male clerk answered. "Looked scared. Ran out the front without saying anything. He turned to the right down the walk."

Fargo didn't take time to thank the clerk but rushed through the store, out the front door, and down the boardwalk. He didn't see the brown suit. So he had to be in another store. A young boy bouncing a ball approached Fargo. He stopped.

"Hey there, boy, did you see a guy in a brown suit run along here and dodge into a store?"

"Sure, he went into the barbershop."

It was two doors down. Fargo ran to the door, opened it, and saw the man wasn't there.

"Hey, you're bleeding," the barber said. "I can fix that for you."

"No time. Did a man in a brown suit run through here?"

"Yep, right out the back door without so much as a howdy. Seemed to be in a rush." He pointed at a draped doorway, and Fargo eased through it, cleared the small room, and then went out the back door into the alley behind the store.

He at once looked at the ground. It had been a dry summer. The dust was an inch thick in the alley. The trail of the man's town boots showed plainly. He had turned left, back the way he had come. Fargo ran, following the footprints.

They went straight down the alley, overprinted a horse and wagon's tracks, and then turned away from town into a jumble of weeds and grass behind three houses. Fargo paused where the trail went into the grass. It was slower going now, but he found the sign where the boots had jolted into the ground, mashing down weeds and bending over the grass. The tracks headed straight for the middle house. Fargo paused and watched the house. There were no windows in back. He ran for it, following the tracks as they led to the left side of the building. He could see two windows and a door.

Fargo crept up to the door, and at the same time a six-gun broke out a small pane in the window four feet in front of the door. A voice yelled at once.

"Don't know how you got this far, Fargo. Don't matter. I got the widow Plateneau in here with her six-year-old girl. You try to come through that door and both of them are dead. You hear me? Be two dead females on your head. I want you to come on around the house to the street and go back around the block to town. I can see you most of the way. You do that now or these two are dead, you hear? Answer me."

The brown suit and bowler. The man he chased had to be Dutch. "I hear you, Dutch. You killed that bald-headed man in his little house, didn't you? Yeah, had to be you, a knife job. Hear you like to use your knife. I'm going. Leave the innocents in there alone. This isn't their battle. It's you and me now, Dutch, just you and me."

There was nothing else Fargo could do. Two more lives were not a fair price for killing Dutch. He'd do just as he said—but he'd come back and watch the house unseen until Dutch left. He knew the killer wouldn't stay there long.

Fargo did as Dutch instructed, only he jogged and he made frequent changes in directions so even a man aiming a rifle would have a hard time staying with him. He kept looking back at the house, and when he could no longer see the back window, where he figured Dutch would be watching from, he paused and worked out a route to the house where he could see both sides of it but not be seen from it. He ran for two more blocks, then came out to the same alley he'd been in before, and found a spot in back of a store where he hid behind some wooden crates. He could see most of the middle house. His guess was that when Dutch left, he would come out the side door and to the rear of the house and walk through the short field to the town alley toward Main Street.

Fargo checked his watch. It was nearly five o'clock. It would be dark in another two hours. He figured Dutch would make his break soon. His one worry was that as soon as Dutch could no longer see him, he had bolted out of the house and had already gone through the alley and back in town. As Fargo waited, he put his handkerchief over the wound on his shoulder. He stuffed it through the tear in his shirt, then unfolded it. The shirt held the makeshift bandage in place. The dull ache from the knife wound began to drill into his brain. He pushed it back, told himself it didn't hurt that bad, and willed himself to control the pain.

He waited until ten minutes after five, when finally he heard the back door slam and saw Dutch come out, checking carefully around the back of the house. Then he ran across the grass and weeds the forty yards toward the alley.

He was fifty feet from Fargo's hiding spot when he

slowed, then shook his head and began running the other way. Fargo took two shots at him, knowing he was out of range of the Colt, but it scared Dutch into running faster.

Fargo jogged after him. Dutch was a sprinter. Fargo guessed that on a measured course the rail-thin guy would outclass him. Now he was running for his life.

There was no easy hiding spot this time. It was three hundred feet to the next cross street, where Dutch turned right, heading back to Main Street. He stayed sixty feet ahead. Fargo put on a surge of speed but couldn't get close enough for a sure shot. He still had three rounds in the Colt and didn't want to have to reload on the fly.

At Main Street, Dutch walked up beside a woman and said something to her, then suddenly grabbed her and turned her so she was in front of him. He waited for Fargo.

When Fargo was forty feet away, he bellowed at him. "Stop right there, Fargo or my knife goes in this one. You stay there and don't move, or I swear I'll kill her." He began backing up toward the store just behind him. It was Sally's Millinery. He pushed in the door, slipped inside, and closed it.

Sally blinked. "Young man—"

"Shut up and sit on the floor," he commanded. "Do it or I'll kill this woman." Sally sat delicately on the wooden floor. He saw the other woman in the shop. "You, too, lady." She went down and began to cry softly.

He looked for the back door. Finding it, he dragged the hostage toward the exit. The woman he held had been crying, but now she set her jaw, and when he loosened his grip, she turned and tried to kick her knee up into his crotch. He closed his legs quickly and her knee missed the mark. He slapped her roughly and pushed her to the back door. Dutch looked out. He saw no one in the alley. Fargo would be at the front door, trying to figure out if he could break in or not. Dutch stepped out the door, then surged back inside. No gunfire. The coast was clear.

"Lady, we're walking out into the alley. If nothing happens, I'll let you go and you won't get hurt. You try to get away again, I'll slit your throat. You understand?"

The hostage wiped tears from her eyes. "Yes, I understand."

They edged out the back door, and as soon as they were clear, Dutch pushed the woman away and sprinted down the long alley to Second Street, which would take him back to Main.

This time Fargo had outguessed him. Fargo had gone back to First Street only four doors down from the millinery shop and moved down the alley until he could see the back door to Sally's, and waited. He saw Dutch test the scene twice, then the third time he came out. As soon as Dutch pushed the woman away, Fargo fired. His first round hit Dutch in the right shoulder. He dodged one way and then the other and kept running. Fargo's second shot missed as he took up the chase. Then it was another footrace. Dutch's left arm hung uselessly at his side. Then he grabbed it and held it across his chest. He bolted into the back door of the Roundhouse Saloon. Dutch vanished inside and Fargo waited a moment at the door. Then he swung it open and stepped to the side. No shots came. Fargo went through low and fast. He was in a hall with four doors opening off it. The first one opened, and the cook came out with a pan of vegetable tops and peelings. She glared at Fargo and his smoking Colt.

He passed her and opened the second door. Storage, nobody there. The third and fourth doors also opened on empty rooms. Ahead was the back stairs to the cribs upstairs. An ideal spot for an ambush. He wondered if Dutch had a revolver. He hadn't seen one. Dutch didn't have a gun belt.

Fargo rushed up the stairs three steps at a time. At the top he threw open the first door and saw two naked bodies bathed in sweat pounding and bouncing on the bed. They never noticed that he was there. He closed the door and went to the next. Empty. In the third one, he found a man just pulling off his pants and a nude woman sitting on the bed.

"Hey, we ain't done yet," the woman snarled. "Wait your fucking turn." Fargo grinned and retreated.

In the hall, two women came from the stairs escorting two men. They stared at him a minute.

"Hurt your shoulder, handsome?" the redhead asked on her way past. He let them go in doors and noticed the ones they didn't use. The woman in another room was taking a bath from a small tub. She turned, her large breasts hanging straight down.

"Hey, I ain't ready yet. You said I had ten minutes for a whore's bath."

He left. The next door was locked. He knocked on it. Nobody answered. He had covered all the rooms except two. The one next door was empty. Fargo loaded the empty chambers in his Colt, then came back to the locked door and kicked hard with his boot at the spot right beside the knob. The lock flew apart and the door swung inward. A shot snarled from inside, small-caliber from the sound of it. Fargo had jumped to the left when the door caved open, and the shot missed. He heard a girl scream. Fargo surged around the door jamb leading with his six-gun.

Dutch looked up, a single-shot Derringer in his hand and his face a sad grin. "Fargo, I just cut this girl bad on the leg. I hit a major vein. If you hold the sides together hard, she won't bleed to death. All you have to do is put your gun on the floor, come over here, and hold the sides of the cut. If you don't I'll cut her jugular and she'll be dead in five minutes. Your choice."

Fargo bent and put his Colt on the floor, then slid it under the bed so the knife man couldn't pick it up.

Dutch chuckled. "Smart, yeah, you're real smart. I didn't even think of that. Come on over here now. I'm going past you. Don't touch me. Agreed?"

Fargo nodded. They changed places and Fargo grabbed the woman's leg and held the wound together. It ran with thick blood. The woman had fainted. He pressed a wad of the bedding on it, forcing it against the wound hard to stop the flow of blood.

Dutch vanished out the door.

Fargo bellowed. "Somebody get in here and help me. This woman has been cut bad."

A redheaded woman in a robe looked in the door. "Ruth!" she shrieked.

"Send someone quick for the doctor," Fargo bellowed.

Ten minutes later, the doctor had treated the cut on Ruth's leg, and she was out of danger. The big brassy redhead who Fargo had seen at the door cornered him.

"What happened here? I need to know."

Fargo told her of his chase and how it had ended here with Dutch cutting Ruth.

"That bastard. He's cut a girl before on me. I told him never to come back. He's just plain bad. I'll tell the sheriff, but I think Crosby is afraid to do anything to Dutch. Thanks for helping Ruth." She smiled, and her makeup almost cracked. "Hey, you want a free one? Pick out any girl who takes your fancy. Wanda pays her debts, and she owes you one."

Fargo grinned. "Wanda, maybe later. Right now I've got too much to get done."

Outside the Roadhouse Saloon, Fargo headed for the train station. He wanted to report what had happened today, especially about Dutch trying to bushwhack him. He was only halfway there when Sheriff Crosby waved at him.

"You better see this. Somebody cut up a guy and a whore real bad over in the Whisper Saloon about an hour ago. It might have something to do with the train robbery. Doc Andrews patched up the girl and she should make it, but the man was stone cold dead and blood all over the place. Some of the girls say it was Dutch who did it. They saw him go up the stairs with this Frazer guy and Kelly."

When Fargo heard Dutch's name, he ran. He beat the sheriff to the scene and vaulted up the stairs. One of the girls pointed at Kelly's room. The girl was in bed. The place had been cleaned up, with new sheets and a quilt on the bed and the blood mostly mopped up from the floor. The man's body had been removed. Kelly was awake, but looked pale and shaken.

"Kelly, was it Dutch who cut you?" Fargo asked. She nodded.

"Why did he do it?"

"He didn't find what he wanted. Said he was looking for something."

Talking tired her and Fargo waited. The sheriff came in the door and listened.

"Dutch was hunting for something. Did he say what?"

"He kept yelling at Nate to find the will. He said, find the will or you're a dead man."

"They were looking for it here?"

"Nate told me he had it when he was here two nights ago, and evidently he lost it somewhere. But they didn't find it."

"Thanks, Kelly. You rest now. Looks like you're going to be fine in a few weeks."

"Not fine, not really." She pointed to the bandage on her cheek. "Doc Andrews says I'll have a scar on my cheek. I'm out of business here. You ever see a whore with a scarred-up face? I know that as soon as she can, Josie will throw me out. Then what will I do?"

"Don't worry about that now. Just rest and get your strength back and get well."

The two men left. Josie, the madam, followed them downstairs. The sheriff took off and Fargo turned to the woman. He took fifty dollars out of his purse and handed it to Josie. "You take care of Kelly. This should pay her way for six months. If I hear that Kelly's not getting the best treatment, I'll come back here and do some housecleaning, starting with you, Josie."

"Hey, no need to get nasty. I always take care of my

girls. She can stay until she's well. Now git, you're bad for business."

Outside, the sheriff had waited for Fargo. "I've got a warrant for Dutch's arrest for the killing and the knife work on Kelly," the sheriff said. "We'll find him, and hang him. I've got men watching every train." He paused. "What happened to your shoulder?"

"One of Dutch's throwing knives. We had a little chase, and he wound up cutting Ruth."

"Better see the doc."

"Yeah. Right now. The sawbones has had a busy day."

After Doc Andrews treated and bandaged the stab wound in his shoulder, Fargo sat in a chair in the fading light in front of the hardware store. Sarah Wellford walked by and stopped.

"You're hard at work, I see," she said.

He stood and grinned. "Trying to put this all together."

"I just heard about Kelly. Is she going to live?"

"Should, unless something unexpected happens. Doc said she should make it. She said Dutch was looking for the will in her room. Running this kid all over town looking for it."

"Left it in her room? Did they find it?"

"Nope. They tore the place apart, then Dutch killed the kid. Kelly called him Nate."

Sarah frowned. "Looking for something left in her room by one of her customers, you say. Hey, I'm doing a story on her, and she brought me a whole box full of things that men have left, including some big envelopes."

Fargo caught her arm. "Let's go take a look. That will was probably the whole reason for the train robbery."

A few minutes later in the newspaper office, Sarah picked up a cardboard box and put it on her desk. She took out three envelopes and opened the first one. It contained some kind of hardware order forms. The second one held some personal papers. The third one had a thick pad of paper held together with staples.

"Last will and testament of . . ." Sarah looked up. "This must be the will Dutch was hunting for, and the same one that Kirk Gaylord is after."

Fargo sat on the edge of her desk and watched her. "So what are you going to do with it? It's stolen property, you realize."

"Yes, I know that." There was an edge in her voice, a new hardness he hadn't heard before. "This newspaper is extremely short on funds. I'm almost broke. Dad was a great newspaper man but not much of a businessman. I need a new press, more type fonts, another type cabinet, and a folder. I'd think any ordinary citizen who found this will would be entitled to a reward. Especially since the will is worth a million and a half dollars to Mr. Kirk Gaylord."

"A reward would be reasonable," Fargo said.

"I do need twenty thousand dollars to get this paper on a firm foundation and with some operating money. In another year I'll be earning my way and maybe making a small profit." She sighed and threw the will on the desk. "The trouble is, I can't demand a reward. That would be illegal. It is stolen property." She frowned and stared at him. "You work for the railroad. Aren't you obligated to grab the will and turn it over to the post office as recovered material from the train robbery?"

"Probably," Fargo said. "Actually, I've never seen any paper that I could swear was the missing Gaylord will. So what can I do? On the other hand, we might be able to use the will to smoke out one big rat in this whole robbery scheme."

"I don't understand."

"We tell Kirk Gaylord that you found the will and will give it back to him tonight outside of town. With that bait, good old Dutch should be hellbent on grabbing the will for his side."

"So, we go see Mr. Gaylord and see if he'll go along with the plan. Why don't I just take the will to his office?"

"Because we need it to nail Dutch. He's killed five people already. I'll be there to take care of him. But we need the will as bait."

Ten minutes later, Kirk Gaylord grabbed Sarah and gave her a big hug. "You found it, you wonderful, wonderful woman. I might just ask you to marry me. When do I get the will?" He hesitated. "Oh, I've told various people around town there's a reward. I didn't mention any figure, but that's a tremendously valuable piece of paper to me. I'm thinking of twenty-five thousand dollars."

"That would be wonderful."

"Just one little complication," Fargo said. He outlined the plan to Kirk, who frowned at first but then agreed to the plan to lure Dutch out into the open. "One more thing. Tell your lawyer from St. Louis the good news about the meeting tonight."

Kirk frowned. "I don't understand why. But I'll do all of it. Just so I have the will by tomorrow morning at ten o'clock for that hearing. The judge moved it up on us."

"You can have it tonight," Fargo said. "Come to the stagecoach station about three miles east outside town on the old road at eight o'clock tonight. Sarah will be there with the will."

Kirk shook Sarah's hand, then kissed it. "Young lady, you're the answer to my prayers. I'll be there tonight. Watch out for Dutch. I heard he's still hunting for the will."

"I'll be there," Sarah said, and she and Fargo left. "Now all I have to do is be sure the will is safe for the next few hours."

An hour later, Kirk Gaylord told his lawyer from St. Louis, Ormly Quant, about the marvelous stroke of luck. Quant nodded, then smiled. "Well, that sets up the reading of the true will tomorrow. All we have to do is show up, and the bulk of the estate is yours." Quant excused himself shortly and went down the street. He searched two saloons and almost gave up. In the worst saloon in town, the Whisper Saloon, he found Dutch hiding in a far corner. Dutch's trademark brown suit and bowler were gone. He wore old jeans, a blue shirt, and a cap that covered half his face.

Quant sat down beside him. "Sheriff is looking for you," Quant said. Dutch nodded and emptied the shot glass in front of him. He at once filled it again from a bottle of rot gut. Quant grabbed the bottle and the shot glass. "No more booze. I've got a job for you that could mean we'll all collect that twenty-five thousand dollars after all."

Precisely at eight o'clock, Sarah Wellington sat in a one-horse surrey in front of the abandoned stagecoach station. The stage had made its last run a week after the railroad finished laying track into Plainview. There was a small barn for hay, a stable for ten horses, and the station house, just a shack for the station boss to eat and sleep in between his job of changing horses on the stages and keeping the spare nags fed and in good health.

Fargo had ridden the Ovaro beside the surrey from town but turned off a quarter of a mile from the coach house. He circled around and came in behind it, then dismounted and eased into a position thirty feet from the parked surrey. Sarah actually had three identical envelopes. The real will was under her feet. An envelope with blank legal paper was in her hand, and behind her on the seat was another fake will envelope. Depending who showed up, she would determine which envelope she gave out.

Soon a horse came galloping in. It skidded to a stop near her. Dutch, not Kirk Gaylord, swung down from the horse and leaped into the surrey beside her.

"Give me the will," he demanded. She gave him the envelope she held. He growled at her, jumped from the surrey, and got on his horse. Then he looked inside the envelope. Even in the pale moonlight he could see that the pages were blank. He vaulted off the horse again. The round from Fargo's Colt dug up dirt just in front of his boots as he started for the surrey.

"Far enough, Dutch. You and I have a score to settle."

Dutch turned and pulled out a revolver and shot four times where he thought the voice came from.

"Bad idea, Dutch, now you only have one round left."

Dutch jumped into the surrey, grabbed the reins, and slapped them on the horse's back. The surrey jolted off with the horses at a gallop.

Fargo mounted the Ovaro and chased them. The rig hurtled away from town. The Ovaro was faster and caught the surrey two hundred feet down the old stage road. When he was twenty feet behind the rig, Fargo fired one round past the side where Dutch was driving. The killer leaned out and fired back, his last round unless he had reloaded. Fargo fired once more. The rough road caused the surrey to bounce and shift to one side. Fargo's round missed Dutch's shoulder and dug into the rear end of the horse. The frightened animal panicked and galloped flat-out.

A runaway.

Fargo swore at himself and spurred the Ovaro after the wild-eyed, out-of-control horse. It tore down the old stage coach road, made a skidding turn, and then headed for a downslope. The black had no thought but to get away from the stinging pain in its rear haunch. It ran full tilt on the downslope and didn't see the curve ahead. She ran straight off the edge of the road. The surrey bounced on its big wheels once. Then a wheel broke and it tipped, breaking free from the traces, and tumbled and rolled down the slope for thirty feet.

Fargo rode down cautiously, watching for any sign of Dutch or Sarah. He found Sarah close to the old road. She must have tumbled out on the first bounce of the rig. She sat up clutching two envelopes.

"I still have the will," she whispered. Then she tried to move her right arm and screeched in pain. Fargo looked at it in the dim light.

"Broken," he said. "Looks like between your wrist and elbow. You hang tight here while I find Dutch."

A shot whined past Fargo from less than thirty feet away. Fargo could tell by the sound the gun made. He knew that Dutch had reloaded. Fargo fired in Dutch's direction as he ran to the left away from Sarah.

"You'll never find me in the dark, Dutch. How badly hurt are you?"

"I'm not hurt at all and I have a hundred rounds, so don't worry about me running out of ammo."

Fargo adjusted his aim to where he thought the voice came from. Then he fired four quick shots into the area. A cry of pain came from Dutch.

"Bastard," Dutch roared. "You damned bastard, I'm gonna kill you slow."

Fargo had moved right after he fired. He reloaded and angled closer to Dutch, working through the faint moonlight, staying close to the ground, not making a sound. He found a rock and threw it behind where he figured the knife man lay. The clunk of the rock brought two shots in that direction from Dutch.

Fargo moved forward again as the sound of the shots faded. Then he stopped and listened. Dutch must have been thrown out of the surrey on the second roll. He was farther down the slope. Fargo threw a rock in front of Dutch but well away from Sarah. The sound brought two more rounds from Dutch's gun. That pinpointed his location for Fargo. He was only ten feet away. Fargo could see the edge of a large boulder. The killer must be behind it or on its far side.

The boulder made his job harder, but it did give an advantage too. It screened Dutch, but it also blinded him so he couldn't tell what Fargo was doing. He had to go forward. He held his cocked Colt in hand and wormed forward toward the rock on his belly, pushing himself with his feet and pulling with his elbows.

"What the hell you doing, Trailsman?" Dutch called, his voice quavering.

After two minutes, Fargo had crept up to the boulder without alerting the gunman. Fargo crawled up on the three-foot high boulder and lifted his Colt. He could see Dutch's arm and hand holding a six-gun beyond the boulder.

Fargo shot Dutch's right wrist, smashing half a dozen bones, blasting the pistol out of his hand. Dutch wailed in protest. "Shoulda killed you early on. They wouldn't let me. Shoulda done it."

Fargo stared down at the man. "Dutch, I figure you killed at least five people now. For that the state of Missouri can hang you only once. But I can make you hurt one hell of a lot before you walk up that scaffold." Fargo wanted to punish the killer, to shoot him in the shoulder and kneecap. But he held off. He moved up and saw Dutch's twisted right leg. It had to be broken.

Fargo heard a rider coming. He flattened out near the boulder, quickly reloading the Colt.

"Hello, anyone here?" a voice called. "Sarah, are you out here? I'm Kirk Gaylord. We were supposed to meet back at the old stage post. Then I heard the shooting."

Fargo stood. "We're here, Gaylord. I'm coming out to the road. We need a buggy or a wagon. Dutch is here with a broken leg and he got shot, but he's still alive. Sarah has a broken arm."

Once he'd returned to the road, Fargo helped Sarah stand and they went to the Ovaro. He perched her on his saddle and walked her up to where Kirk sat on his mount.

"Dutch was out here? How did he know we were meeting here?"

"Who did you tell about the meeting to get the will?"

"Only one I told was my lawyer . . . my God, Quant's been working for Terrance all along. That low-down, cheating son of a bitch."

"Happens," Fargo said. "Sarah, do you have something for this gentleman?"

Sarah handed Kirk the envelope. He opened it and checked quickly.

"Yes, thank God, that's the will. Here's my draft to you for twenty-five thousand dollars. You really earned your reward."

"Mr. Gaylord, I know we talked about a reward, but I can't accept it. It seems like a ransom. It's simply not right."

Gaylord frowned and shook his head. "You mean you're going to give me the will for nothing?"

"I found the will when working on a story. I'm a journalist and I have my integrity to consider. My father taught me that a long time ago."

Gaylord stepped down from his mount and walked up to where Sarah sat on the Ovaro. "Young lady, I owe you a deep debt for finding the will. It means a great deal of money to me. But I talked to several people offering a reward for the return of the will. I too have my integrity to consider. I couldn't hold up my head in town if I don't give the reward. Your journalistic integrity is in no way compromised. Call it a gift to the newspaper so you can buy that new press I know you need. Please accept the gift, donation, whatever you want to call it. My integrity demands it."

Sarah's eyes went wide. "I never thought of it that way. I guess . . . I mean, now that you put it that way, it really doesn't hurt my journalistic standing. Yes, I'll accept. Thank you, Mr. Gaylord."

"Thank you, Miss Wellford."

Fargo motioned to Gaylord. "One more thing. You see that boulder over there about thirty yards? That's where Dutch is. Can you go into town and bring back a wagon to haul his worthless carcass to the sheriff? He has a broken leg, and I don't know where his horse ran off to. The sheriff has an arrest warrant for Dutch."

"Least I can do, Fargo. I'm off and riding."

Fargo eased up on the saddle behind Sarah. "We'll go into town carefully, right to Dr. Andrews' office," Fargo said. "Looks like you're going to need some help delivering your papers."

Just after the doctor finished setting Sarah's arm, a wagon stopped out front. He went to look at his next patient. He came back shaking his head.

"That man Dutch has a broken leg and he's been shot. Wonder how that happened. He's next. You're about done, young lady. No working with that arm for at least three weeks. Then we'll see how it's coming along."

Sarah scowled and stared at Fargo. "How am I going to put out a newspaper if I can't work with my left hand? Who is going to write the stories? Who is going to set the type? Nobody in town but me can run that press. I'm going to have to skip two issues?"

"Hey, we'll think of something. Maybe there's an old printer in town who can set type. We'll put up a notice on the town bulletin board and on all the stores. You can still write the stories with your right hand. Besides, you told me the current issue is about ready. We'll make do."

11

Fargo and Sarah made do at her cottage. First Fargo cooked dinner: fried potatoes and onions, then added grated cheese that melted over the concoction. That, with strips of bacon, cut-up string beans, and coffee with toast and strawberry jam, made their menu.

"Why didn't you tell me you could cook?" Sarah asked. "I might hire you full-time."

"I could be here waiting for you when you came from your job at the paper."

"Something like that." She reached over and kissed him between bites of the delicious potatoes and onions.

"That splint on your arm will bother you for at least two days. By then you'll forget it's there and be back doing everything you used to do. I still think you need a back shop man to set type and headlines and run the press."

"Yeah, and now I can afford to hire one. I'll start looking around. The newspapers in the state have a network."

After dinner Fargo put on his hat and adjusted his Colt. He had spent a half hour cleaning and oiling it after they got to her house.

"I have a small job to do. I still want to catch that kid who's been spending the robbery money. If we can nail him, we should have his dad cold stone dead for the robbery."

"I'll go with you."

138

"Might be better if I went alone. I'm going to be just sitting watching some of the stores that stay open late."

"That's no fun. We can have more fun here," she purred.

"After I get back. I'll need some relaxing."

"Promise?"

"Promise."

In the coal-black dark, Fargo spent a half hour across the street from the general store. He watched everyone who went in and out. Then he remembered the back door, and slid around the end of the street and up the alley. He found a spot one door down among some discarded boxes and settled in. This was the best store for the kid to hit again. Since he hadn't been seen on the street, he must use the stores' back doors. After five o'clock, a part-time clerk usually was on duty, and might not even know to watch for the pimply-faced fourteen-year old boy.

After an hour of waiting, Fargo wanted to get up and stretch. But he didn't. He'd seen Indians cover themselves with sand and vanish into a dry river bottom. When an expected enemy tribe showed up in a march to a new campground, a hundred warriors rose on both sides of the long string of their horses, travois, women, and children. They killed two dozen warriors and carried off a hundred horses and ten women. He tried it once with his Indian friend. He lasted only two hours before he rose. But he learned that by hiding and becoming part of the surrounding landscape often helped catch your prey unaware.

Ten minutes before the store's nine o'clock closing time, Fargo sensed movement in the alley. He looked across at the back of the general store and saw a shadow move among some boxes. He had no idea how long the person had been hiding there.

A moment later a small figure, maybe five feet tall, rose from the boxes and hurried to the general store door and inside. It could have been a kid. Fargo rose from his hiding spot and ran silently to the door. He looked inside the storage area. No one there. At the door into the front, he paused and looked around. The same short figure was now at a glass display case toward the front. Inside were revolvers and a rifle. The boy talked to the clerk.

Fargo crept into the store silently, angled behind some tall displays and toward the front where the glass case stood. He took a quick look. Yes, a boy, maybe fourteen, with pimples on his face. He was holding a six-gun. Had to be the kid. Fargo stood and walked toward the case, careful not to look at the boy. He was almost there when the kid dropped the six-gun and darted for the rear door.

Fargo cut him off, tripped him, and pinned him to the floor as the boy wailed and screamed, then kicked the floor with his feet and pounded it with his fists. The clerk stood by with his mouth open.

"He trying to buy a six-gun?"

"Yep, had the money, too."

Fargo dug into the boy's pockets and came out with a roll of new twenty-dollar bills. He figured more than five hundred dollars worth. "Stolen money. You know who this kid is?"

"Oh, yeah, knew him before he went to boarding school back in St. Louis. That's Thornton Neville, the district manager's kid. His dad runs the railroad in this section."

Neville! The name pounded at Fargo like a thunderbolt. The kid must have found stolen money his father was keeping until it cooled off in a year or two.

"Thanks," Fargo said. He stood, jerked the boy up by the back of his collar, and marched him out of the store and across to the county courthouse and the sheriff. A deputy said Sheriff Crosby was home eating dinner, but he'd get him right away. In the meantime, Fargo pushed Neville's kid into a cell and slammed the door shut, locking it.

This was getting more interesting by the minute. Neville must be in on it with Quant, Dutch, and Terrance Gaylord. Had the three of them set up the robbery? Dutch had done the killing and would have probably got a sizable cut along with Quant and Neville once Terrance was assured of his extra eight hundred thousand dollars. Only how could Fargo prove it?

The sheriff stormed into the office ten minutes later. "Neville's kid? You sure? I thought all of them were at boarding schools in St. Louis. What has the boy said?"

"Not a word since I grabbed him trying to buy a six-gun. Look at the roll of bills he had in his pocket." Fargo gave the sheriff the wad, and Crosby whistled. "Damn, must be six or seven hundred dollars here. Let's see what the boy has to say."

But the Neville boy would not say a word. He wouldn't even tell them his name.

"So this brings Neville into it, robbing his own railroad," Crosby said. "He knew the schedules, and what went by registered mail, and he must have known about the shipment of gold and greenbacks. Only how do we prove this? The actual robbers are dead. The men who killed them and brought the gold and goods here were probably paid off and sent east on the train. We've got Dutch. If he'll talk to save his neck from the gallows, we might have a case. Looks like Neville brought the wrong man in to track down the train robbers."

"We still have to prove it," Fargo said. "I was thinking of an idea yesterday. I want to get the three of them together talking about it where we could listen. Neville, Terrance, and Quant. Round up three young boys who can deliver messages. Each of the crooks will think the other called the meeting. Let's make it at Terrance's room at the hotel at ten o'clock."

"How can we hear?" Sheriff Crosby asked.

"Those walls are paper-thin. We get the room next to them and glue our ears to the wall. We should be able to hear enough so three of us can testify and convict them."

Sheriff Crosby sent a deputy out to round up three boys and bring them back to the jail. Fargo had the notes done. He wrote them in pencil on blank paper. They each said the same thing. "Dutch is in jail. We need to have a meeting. Terrance's room tonight at 10 p.m."

By then it was almost nine-thirty. For fifty cents the boys promised they would hunt down the three men until they found them.

"What if it doesn't work?" the sheriff asked.

"Then we'll go with what we can wring out of Dutch. Let's go give it a try."

Dutch was sleeping. Sheriff Crosby woke him up with a dipper full of cold water in his face. He came up sputtering and let out two short screams when he rolled on his shot-up wrist. He shook his head and wiped off the water, then stared at Fargo.

"You should have killed me. You can't prove I did a damned thing. I went up the steps to the whore's room, but nobody saw me stab the kid."

"Kelly did."

"They told me Kelly died."

"She didn't, and she's already given the sheriff a complete statement on what happened, including how you murdered Frazer."

"So?"

"So that means you hang for murder. Unless . . ." Fargo left it open.

"Yeah, unless what, Fargo?"

"Unless you give us details on the train robbery. How Neville staged it, who he hired, what happened to the two errand boys who brought the gold and money and registered mail to Plainview."

"Yeah, I know some of it. You give it to me in writing that I won't hang?"

"I can do that," the sheriff said. " 'Course some judge might overrule me, but I think with the judges I know, they'll go along. Can you write, Dutch?"

"Hell yes. You think I'm ignorant?"

The sheriff brought a pad of lined paper and three sharp

pencils with soft lead and put them down on a small table he carried into the cell.

"We ask you questions. You write down the question and then the answer. Understand?"

"Yeah, yeah. I don't want to stretch no damn hemp. I'll give you chapter and verse, Sheriff, right down to the penny and no bullshit."

Fargo started. "Dutch, who set up the train robbery?"

Dutch wrote the question. "Hell, Neville, Quant, and Terrance Gaylord planned it out. Then Neville set it up, finding the right men."

"Those right men were murdered by the two delivery men who brought the goods to Plainview?" He paused while Dutch scribbled quickly.

"Right, I don't know the names of any of the four. Two dead, two spending their money in St. Louis."

The questioning went on for nearly a half hour. Then Fargo looked at his town watch and pointed at the door.

"Be back soon to continue this," the sheriff said.

They jogged to the Hallmark Hotel, where Terrance was staying, walked up the back steps quietly, and went into the room beside Terrance's. They could hear men talking. They put their ears to the wall and listened. They could make out the words easily. Terrance was talking.

"I still say this thing has unraveled on us. From what Quant here says, Kirk has the new will and the game is over. What we have to do is cut our losses and get out of this as gracefully and with as few law problems as possible."

"Yeah, with Dutch in jail? He's the kind who will spill everything he knows to save his neck from a noose." That was Quant.

Neville chimed in. "What can he prove? Most of it's his word against ours. Evidence, men, the sheriff will need evidence. I can't see where he has much."

"The sheriff has five dead men," Quant said. "The trainman killed by the two dead men doesn't count. That leaves four. You gents heard of criminal conspiracy? That's what we did. Any conspirator can be charged with murder if there is any killing involved in the conspiracy."

"We could all hang?" Terrance whined. "I'm on the morning train."

Neville snorted. "Terrance, this all started with you. It was all your idea. It didn't work. Now we have to figure out how we can take as little blame as possible. By now Kirk knows that Quant was working both ends. Terrance might be able to plead that he authorized no killings, that he did conspire to rob the train, but that was all. Three to five years in prison, I'd guess. So far as I can see, nobody can tie me into this mess. I'm free and clear. There's no evidence, and if you two don't keep your mouths shut about me, I'll hire a man to hunt down both of you and kill you as slowly as possible."

"You're a real bastard, Neville. Now, it's about time we split that twenty-six thousand in gold and greenbacks three ways," Terrance said. "That would be about eight thousand seven hundred each."

"Maybe Neville has spent it all already," Quant said bitterly.

"Not a cent, I haven't spent a cent except for that thousand we paid the two delivery men."

"Then how come the sheriff has picked up seven or eight of the twenty-dollar bills spent here in town?" Quant asked.

"What?" Neville cried.

The sheriff nodded at his deputy and Fargo. "Let's go into the hall, move in, and take them right now," he whispered.

The three got into position quietly. Then Fargo kicked in the door and the three men barged in with guns drawn.

"Hold it, you three. You're all under arrest for murder, train robbery, robbery of U.S. registered mail, conspiracy to commit murder and robbery, and half a dozen more charges when we get them worked out."

The three men were stunned.

"You've been listening to us?" Quant asked.

"Yes, it's been fascinating," Fargo said. Neville drew a hideout Derringer and waved it before he charged for the door. Two shots hit him in the legs, and he went down and the hideout .22 two-shot skittered out of his hand.

The deputy searched the other two men, found two more Derringers and a knife. Then the sheriff herded them down to the jail. He threw Quant and Neville into one cell and Terrance Gaylord in with Dutch. The sheriff sent a deputy to bring Dr. Andrews to take care of Neville's shot-up legs.

The sheriff took Dutch out to the front office, where he continued telling Crosby everything he knew about the operation, writing as he went. They kept at it until well past midnight.

Then Fargo had another question. "Dutch, what about the man who accepted the goods at that small house, the one who you called Baldy. Was it part of the plan for him to die as well?"

"Oh, yes, he would have been a weak link in an otherwise perfect chain from robbery to the three of them."

"Just how did Baldy die, Dutch?"

Dutch hesitated. "Tell you the truth, Fargo, I'd rather not talk about that."

Crosby let it slide. They had more than enough with his testimony and the statements Fargo and the lawman at the hotel would make. Fargo wrote quickly his recollections of the dialogue among the three men in the hotel room. It was well after two a.m. when he finished. He gave the pages to the sheriff and went back to the cottage where he had left Sarah.

She was up, reading and correcting proofs. "I had to do something," she said. "We're still going to be at least a week behind even if you help me the next four days," she said.

"We?"

"Yes, that's what you told me. You said that 'we' would get the paper out somehow." She smiled at him and patted the spot beside her on the bed. "Tell me about what you've been doing for the past five or six hours."

He told her and she smiled. "So, the great train robbery is all solved. What about the twenty-six thousand dollars?"

"Working on that tomorrow, or rather later today. We'll tear Neville's house apart if the kid won't tell us where his dad hid the money and the gold."

"So, from all that you said, you're out of work."

"You might say that."

"Good. Now since you're not working for anyone, it's time you had a small vacation. You can take it right here. No charge for room and board if you continue to make breakfast. Only one other small problem. I've been restless lately. I want you to help reduce my tensions. Now get your clothes off and slip in here between the sheets and let's see if you can release my pent-up stress."

"How long has this problem been bothering you?"

"Let's see. I think since sometime about three a.m. last night. It's much worse now."

"That's up to me to decide."

Sarah slipped out of bed. She was naked. Fargo marveled at her luscious curves, the heft of her full breasts, the flush of her smooth skin.

"Been waiting for you. Don't move. I'll do the honors with your clothes. One of my fantasies is undressing a man, stripping him down one garment at a time until he's raw, buck naked and throbbing. Ready?"

She kissed him first, her tongue darting into his open mouth, working around, discovering new places. Then she kissed his nose and both eyes, then loosened his gun belt and put it carefully on the floor.

"I hear these things can go off if they are dropped," she said.

"True, but I've been known to go off suddenly, too."

She laughed and unbuttoned his buckskin shirt. There was nothing under it. She stripped it off his arms and let her fingers wallow in the bushy black hair on his chest. She rubbed his male breasts and teased his nipples, sucking on them and nibbling them tenderly.

"Yes, I think this is going to work. I bet you can get me aroused if you work at this for a half hour or more."

She hit him in the shoulder with her fist and flashed him a wicked smile. "I'm trying my best."

His hands caught her breasts and massaged them around and around. Then before she could stop him, he bent and sucked on her full melons, bringing from her a gushing surge of fast breathing.

"Now stop that, it's my party first, and your pants are still on."

She worked the buttons on the buckskins and let them fall to the floor. Sarah stepped back and looked at him standing there naked. His manhood had answered the call and stood tall and ready. Sarah caught it and worked it back and forth, then knelt in front of him and sucked him into her mouth, pushing almost all of him inside until she felt him touch deep in her throat. Then she bobbed back and forth until he caught her head and lifted her away.

His voice was husky with potent desire as he moved her to the bed. "Not quite yet, Lady Sarah. Let's save that part for the last act in our little drama."

He grabbed her and they dropped onto the bed. She rolled on top of him and lay there, nibbling his lips, then his tongue. She freed one hand and rubbed gently up and down the inside of his thighs, then caught his erection and pumped it hard.

"Whoa, whoa, there. Can't we find a better place for the stallion down there?"

She laughed softly, moved over him until she was in the best position, then guided him into her heated core, jolting down in one quick thrust with her hips until he was firmly in place.

"Now, that wasn't so hard," she said. "I've got a couple more ideas I want to try before we get too tired."

He pushed his hand between their bodies until he found her hard node, and he drummed on it a dozen times until her gasps and heavy breathing turned into a low wail.

"Yes, yes, yes, yes, yes. So good, so wonderful." Then she was overcome with a shuddering surge that left her panting and yelping. She gave out a long, thin keening moan as her hips drove at him a dozen times before she gave a deep sigh and let herself totally relax. She dropped on him, flowing over him and settling into every part of him until they felt like one being with two minds and only one body. For several minutes she couldn't talk. She at last reached forward and kissed him. Her lips faintly touched his like a butterfly's wings. Then she closed her eyes and smiled.

She roused a moment later and looked down at him. "Your turn," she said. She lifted off him slightly, held herself up on her knees, then began to bounce her hips up and down, taking him fully into her creamy sheath, working him around and up and down with her hips until he wanted to blast upward with his hips. He contained himself and let her work harder and harder. Then before he could stop it, he did explode and so did she again.

"Again," she breathed. She rolled off him and went up on her hands and knees. "Let's do it this way," she said. "Then the next time I have a really wicked idea, and I bet you have two or three yourself."

He did.

It was almost daylight when they kissed one last time and settled down to sleep.

Sarah didn't hear him get up and dress as the sun rose. He looked at his watch and smiled. He knew the time like he knew his own body. He rose with the sun and knew its every position in the sky. He had no need for a watch. He was, after all, the Trailsman. Fargo placed the pocket watch gently on the nightstand. He washed his face and slid on his hat and buckled his gun belt on. He was going to meet the sheriff and go through Neville's house hunting for the money.

At the courthouse, Fargo walked into the sheriff's office and found him ready to go.

"Talked to the kid this morning. Brought him some breakfast from the Farm House Café. He was so hungry he told me where he found the money in his father's bedroom. Ready to go?"

The Neville house was empty and quiet when they went in ten minutes later. The cash and gold were right where the boy told them it would be: in a hollow in the floorboards under the bed. Two panels had been removed, a section a foot wide and two feet long had been built in, and the panels put back so it couldn't be noticed.

Inside they found three of the four boxes of currency still full. The fourth was open and an inch or more of the bills was gone. The two gold bars lay under the boxes of twenties. Beside the bills was an envelope. Inside, they found five bearer bonds, each worth a thousand dollars.

"So, Mr. Delano will get his bonds back, after all," Fargo said. They found a large box and put the money, bonds, and gold in it, then carried it back to the bank, where they banged on the door until the banker opened it.

"Well, now that's what I call a deposit," the banker said, gazing at the money and gold.

"Keep it in your vault until I can turn it over to the proper postal inspector," the sheriff said. "I'm getting off a telegram this morning. Fargo, you can go see Mr. Delano with the bearer bonds, or better yet, tell him they are here so they don't get lost again. He shouldn't have them lying around his house."

At the jail, they went in to talk to Neville.

"We found the money and gold," Fargo said.

"It's all back where it belongs," the sheriff added. "Now, my problem is, what can I do with your son? He had no way of knowing the money was stolen, so there's no criminal charges against him. I know you don't have a wife or any other kids here. What can I do with him?"

"My sister in St. Louis. She'll take him. Do a better job of raising him than I have. I'll give you her address. I'm sure she'll come out here and pick him up."

"When do I get to see a judge?" Quant yelled. "I want some due process here. I still have rights. When will a judge come into this woebegone excuse for a town?"

"He's due back in about three weeks, Quant. I suggest you spend the time finding yourself a good lawyer. You're going to need one. If you get lucky and escape the noose, you'll spend forty years in federal prison somewhere. You robbed the U.S. Mail. That's a federal offense. Even after you do get hung for murder, the feds might want to jail your dead body for forty years."

In the front office, Sheriff Crosby shook Fargo's hand. "You did most of the work on this one, Fargo. But we did nail the guys at last. They won't be robbing any more trains for a while. Last night I wired St. Louis about Neville. They wired back that a new man will be coming out today to take over the operation of the district manager's office."

Fargo nodded. "I'm sure you will take care of these varmints, Sheriff. Now I've got a will reading to go to over at the courtroom."

Twenty minutes later, the proceedings were under way. They brought Terrance around from jail. He had a huge chain on his legs, and his hands were shackled together. He couldn't look anyone in the eye in the courtroom.

The substitute judge, a local attorney named O'Brien, put on a black robe and went to the bench.

"This is a formal hearing, and a record will be kept." He looked at the court secretary, and she nodded.

"This division court in the county of Pendergast and the city of Plainview is now in session. Alternate Judge James O'Brien presiding. Today we are here to read the will of the late Judson Plowright Gaylord, formally residing in St. Louis, Missouri. Are all parties present?"

He looked up, saw the two Gaylord brothers, and a woman who had just arrived on the 9:55.

"Yes, Your Honor, I'm Ginger Gaylord of St. Louis. These are my brothers."

"Very well, the reading of the will may now proceed. I ask our district attorney to do the honors."

Fargo settled into the chair and listened to the legalese contained in the will, and then perked up when the division of the estate came. It was as Kirk had said. Ginger and Terrance each received a half million, the rest went to Kirk.

"The awarding of the five hundred thousand dollars will be put on indefinite hold until the felony case involving Mr. Terrance Gaylord is resolved. Since the felony had to do with the will, any monies due to the accused will be forfeited back to the estate in the event he is convicted. This hearing is finished."

Kirk went at once to his sister. "Ginger, I know we've never been close, but I'd like to have you come live with me here. It isn't St. Louis, but this is a nice little town, and you can help us start a city library, and bring in a concert for a little bit of culture. It will be a real challenge for you. I'll be glad to help you invest your money, so you won't have any worries there."

Ginger nodded and looked around, still a little confused by the legal proceedings. "Yes, Kirk, that sounds fine. Anything you say. Do you have a house here?"

Fargo faded away and hurried up the street. He figured the millinery shop would be open. Sally was there and smiled at him.

"Well, I haven't seen you since you came in here chasing that killer. Hear you caught him."

"Yes. That's what I want to talk to you about."

A half hour later, Fargo walked into the Whisper Saloon, which was quiet this time of morning. He marched upstairs to Kelly's room and knocked. A faint voice called and he went in. Kelly sat up in bed. She had a dress on and was working on her hair. She still had the bandage on her right cheek, but she looked much better than when Fargo saw her the last time.

"Dr. Andrews tells me that your stab wound wasn't as deep as he had feared and that you're cleared to do some traveling. That is, if you want to."

"Travel? I don't understand."

"I've found a place where you can stay. Of course, you'll have to work to pay for your keep, but I don't think you'll mind that."

"Work? What can I do besides . . . this."

"You remember Sally over at the millinery shop? She says you have a flair for hats and dresses and such, and that she would like for you to come work with her. There's a small living area in back of the store that Sally used to use before she bought her house. You're welcome to stay there."

Kelly cried softly. "She said I could come? She knows me and she still said I could . . . The ladies who come in won't be, you know, angry that I'm there? They won't think I'm tainting their goods or anything?"

"If they do, you should slap their faces," Fargo said. "Or maybe give them a good spanking. It's fine with Sally. She's real good people. Whenever you feel strong enough to move, I'll help."

Kelly jumped out of bed. "How about right now? Everything I own I can put in one small bag."

"You get it put together, I'll talk to Josie."

The madam had been up only a few minutes and didn't have her company face on. She peered at Fargo through a crack in her door.

"What the hell do you want?"

"Kelly is moving out. I want that fifty dollars I gave you back, plus the share of Kelly's earnings that you've been saving. Don't give me any trouble about this, Josie.

Kelly says you have at least three hundred dollars of her money."

"What? Three hundred? She's only been here a year. Hell, how does she figure?"

"I can have Sheriff Crosby up here in ten minutes to help you do the figuring."

Josie snorted. "Always did think of you as a smart-ass do-gooder." She sighed. "What the hell. Three hundred and your fifty. Sounds fair enough. Just don't get Crosby down on me or the whole operation is shot here."

"I won't say a bad word, Josie. Let's see the cash."

A half hour later, Fargo escorted Kelly down Main Street to the front door at Sally's Millinery Shop. Sally ran up and gave Kelly a tender hug.

"Kelly, I'm so glad you're here. I'm excited about what we can do working together. You're so good with a needle and thread. Now, these accommodations aren't deluxe, but I hope you like them."

He handed Sally the three hundred dollars and said it was Kelly's. Maybe later she could help Kelly open a bank account. Fargo faded out the front door.

He stood on the boardwalk a minute. Now, what else did he have to settle up here? As he thought about it, somebody came up and stopped in front of him. He looked down and grinned.

"Betty, haven't seen you for some time."

"Yes, I hear that you've been busy with the robbery and such."

"Right, I've been working late hours."

The awkward pause stretched out.

"I guess you aren't going to be back to see me."

"I'm about ready to move on, Betty. Need to check my mailbox and all."

"From what I hear, it's good what you done for the railroad."

He nodded.

"I guess Miss Sarah is pleased, too. Well, about time I get back home to the farm. Things I should do out there."

"That's good, Betty. You be careful now and take care."

She nodded and walked away from him.

Fargo gave a little sigh of relief and hurried down to the newspaper office. Sarah must be there by now. She was. He found her leaning over a type rack, setting type in the tray one letter at a time. The plaster of paris cast on her arm was smudged with ink. Her cheek had a black mark on it, and she kept blowing errant strands of blonde hair away from her face. She looked up and scowled.

"You really think I could find a typesetter here in town?"

"Or in St. Louis."

"Might try. Come over here. You should learn a type case. All you do is memorize where each letter and figure is in the case. Then you pick it up and spell the word in this little metal tray. Of course it's upside down and backward."

"What happens if you drop the tray?"

"That's called pieing the type and we don't want to do that." She looked up at him. "Did you get Kelly moved like we talked about last night?"

"Sure did. Everything looks good. Even got three hundred dollars out of Josie."

"Amazing. Josie usually is not a soft touch."

"Now you're the only problem I have left."

"How so?"

"Getting you a typesetter-pressman."

"I'm working on it." She frowned. "I have a larger problem."

"What's that?"

"There's nothing to hold you here, and I'm afraid you're going to ride away one of these days."

"You're right. I will have to. It's my job. That's my life."

She grabbed his hand. "Come here." She led him to the front door, which she locked, then to the back door, which she locked, then to the old sofa that she used to sleep on back when money was really short.

"Sit," she said. He did and she sat beside him. "Since you're probably going to ride out of here, I'm going to do what I can to try to get you to stay." She bent and kissed him, then pushed him down on the sofa. "How am I doing so far?" she asked.

"I think you have the right idea. Just keep on trying."

LOOKING FORWARD!
The following is the opening
section from the next novel in the exciting
Trailsman series from Signet:

**THE TRAILSMAN #234
APACHE DUEL**

*West Texas, 1858—The desert is cruel,
even to those born to it. . . .*

Skye Fargo unknotted the red bandanna from around his
neck and squeezed out what seemed to be a quart of sweat.
Mopping his weathered face helped a little but did nothing
to ease the effects of the intensely bright West Texas sun
hammering down unmercifully on him. He prayed for a
breeze to evaporate the sweat that made his shirt stick to his
muscular body like a second skin, but the cruel desert re-
fused. Not even a hint of wind blew across the rolling landscape. Like the promise of shade given by the thorny
mesquite trees lining the long-dry arroyos, such cooling relief was only a lingering lie.

His lake-blue eyes studied the horizon and saw nothing
there but the constant silvery heat shimmering. He turned in
the saddle to look at his back trail. The faithful Ovaro
shifted its weight and whinnied in complaint.

"I know, I know," Fargo said, patting the horse on the
neck. "It's too hot for both of us." He had left Fort Stockton
before dawn, thinking to be well along the road to Fort
Davis before the sun turned the desert into a griddle and

anyone foolish enough to ride across it into a strip of frying bacon.

That had been his plan, but Fargo had not considered the dearth of shelter once on the trail. He had passed an abandoned stagecoach way station a couple hours outside Fort Stockton, but it had hardly been dawn then; so he had kept riding, thinking he would find another suitable place to hole up until the fierce heat died and the sun sank in the west. Travel at twilight was more dangerous since sidewinders and other, bigger predators came out to hunt then, but Fargo got along just fine with them. Mutual respect went a long way in defining territory, and he was always careful not to intrude, especially if the land's occupants had twin fangs capable of injecting poison.

But the sun! He could not avoid it as he would a poison snake. Fargo could only hide from it, and he had passed up that chance because there had not been another building of any sort in view for hours.

The Ovaro nickered and shook its head. Fargo patted its neck again. It wanted water. He had some in a canvas desert bag, but it was for him. And maybe it wasn't going to be enough. Fargo's mouth turned cottony as he lost more and more bodily moisture to sweat. He eyed the desert bag, cool and damp and inviting, but if he drank now, he might find himself in serious need of water farther along the dusty road.

He reached into his pocket and pulled out a small, smooth stone. The man known far and wide as the Trailsman popped it into his mouth and began rolling it around until saliva began to flow. It wasn't much, but it could keep a man alive. Fargo knew it had kept many an Apache alive in temperatures worse than he was enduring now.

Fargo snorted, mopped his forehead, and fastened the bandanna back around his neck again before riding on slowly. Anything the Apaches could do, Fargo could also. He had proved that time and time again.

"Got to be a spot for us to rest," Fargo said, judging that the angle of the sun was working against him. The hot sun beat down directly at the top of his floppy-brimmed black felt hat, meaning it was noon.

He was in no particular hurry, other than to get out of the punishing sun for a spell. Fargo had scouted a bit out of Fort Stockton on a steady drift toward the west. Considering how punishing the sun was, he knew he should have headed northwest from Fort Stockton rather than west in order to get to the Rockies and find a cool, clear running stream on some mountainside. Farther north and west he could lose himself for the entire summer in the Bitterroots. Montana and Idaho were mighty pretty this time of year.

"There it is," he said to his horse, tugging the reins a little to get the Ovaro headed in the right direction. A large ravine had been savagely cut by spring runoff months earlier, leaving a high bank. Not much shadow offered shelter this near noon, but in a half hour he would have a fine spot to nod off and wait for cooler temperatures.

The horse saw nothing to interest it but took little persuading to go where its rider insisted. The Ovaro was well trained and did whatever crazy thing Fargo demanded of it, even riding in the scorching midday summer desert heat.

Barely had the horse eased down the steep, sandy slope when Fargo reined back hard and canted his head to one side, listening hard for the faint sound of gunfire ahead. For a moment Fargo thought he had heard a mirage—if that was possible. If a man could see what wasn't there, why couldn't he hear a ghost gunfight?

The echoes convinced him he was not hallucinating. The gunshots were real. He heaved a sigh, checked the Colt riding at his hip and then the Henry rifle in its saddle sheath. He put his heels to the Ovaro's flanks and got the horse walking faster. To gallop in heat like this would kill the poor animal within a hundred yards.

Riding up the arroyo brought him to a road crossing it at a crazy angle. The spring runoff had cut through the road and made for dangerous passage then and difficult now, thanks to the loose gravel and sand on the ravine floor.

Fresh tracks showed Fargo that at least three wagons had passed within the hour. The sound of nearby gunshots carried an urgency, doubled by the war whoops of Apaches. Some settler had blundered off the main road Fargo had been following and gotten into big trouble with marauding Indians.

The sharp scent of burning wood came to Fargo, borne on a hot wind blowing directly from the west. He gave the Ovaro its head, not wanting to push the horse beyond its limits. There might not be much he could do if the wagon train found itself attacked by fifty Indians—not much more than to reverse his course and return to Fort Stockton for a cavalry detachment. If he had to follow such an unpleasant path, leaving men and women to their fate, he wanted a strong horse able to carry him fast.

But Fargo doubted he would do anything like that, unless all the settlers were dead and all hope was gone. Saving them meant more than capturing the Indian renegades. Turning tail was not the way Fargo figured to rescue them. His hand brushed the solid butt of his Colt, and then he reached level ground.

A quarter mile off, one wagon had broken down, leaving it easy prey for the Mescaleros. They had set fire to the wagon, driving the occupants toward the remaining two wagons. From the bodies on the ground, Fargo knew they had not gotten far before being cut down.

Whoops and rifle fire told him some resistance was being put up by the other two wagons. They tried to keep moving in spite of being under attack. This diverted the attention of at least one in the wagon from the serious job of shooting back at the Apaches.

"No," Fargo groaned when he saw the lead wagon had reached a fatal decision. Rather than park close to the other wagon so they could guard each other's backs and fight more effectively, the driver insanely tried to outrun Indians on horseback.

He paid for this arrogance—or stupidity—quickly. The Indians swarmed around the fleeing wagon and killed the driver and the occupants within a minute, then set to stealing the mules pulling the wagon and looting the contents. Fargo turned his attention to saving the occupants of the remaining wagon. They had wisely stopped so all of them could fight off the circling Apaches, making it harder for the half dozen Indians to lift their scalps and steal their belongings.

Fargo unlimbered the Henry and brought it to his shoulder. The range was greater than he liked, but he was an expert marksman. His Ovaro stood stock-still while he aimed and squeezed off the first round. The report caused the horse to shift a mite; then Fargo got a second shot off. Both found their targets. The first knocked an Apache off his horse, and the second winged one Fargo took to be the war leader.

His unexpected attack caused the Apaches to break off and come for him. As they turned their backs on the settlers, they found themselves being cut down from the rear. Fargo put a few more rounds into the air but found it harder to hit his targets. The Apaches' horses reared and bucked, and the warriors began riding low to avoid his fire.

Fargo fell into a steady rhythm of aim, squeeze, fire. He methodically sent leaden death winging toward the Indians until the Henry's magazine came up empty. Replacing the rifle in its sheath, Fargo saw that more drastic action was needed if he wanted to save the settlers. The Apaches were not breaking off and running, as he had expected when he began taking potshots at them.

Drawing his Colt, he took a deep breath to settle himself. For good measure, he whipped out his Arkansas toothpick and waved it above his head so the blade caught the sunlight and reflected the death he sought to inflict.

"Hi-yaaa!" Fargo screeched at the top of his lungs. Knife waving in one hand and pistol in the other, he guided his horse using only his knees. The Ovaro charged straight into the center of the tight knot of Apaches, who were trying to decide what to do, who to attack, how to do it.

Fargo got off three rounds from his six-shooter before the Indians broke and ran. They galloped hell-bent for leather, him on their heels until it was obvious they were not going to regroup and attack again. Fargo stopped the frantic run and pulled the horse to a halt, kicking up dust as it dug in its heels.

He resheathed his Arkansas toothpick and shoved his six-gun into its holster before riding slowly toward the wagon. To be sure they didn't mistake him for a road agent come to rob them after the Apaches finished their attack, Fargo held his hands up over his head.

"Hello, are you all right?" he called. "The Apaches hightailed it out of here. You're safe now."

Fargo expected a response: a heartfelt thanks, an angry growl, or even a bullet intended to keep him at bay. Coldness knotted in his gut when he neared the wagon and no one responded in any way. He feared he had arrived too late to save the settlers.

"Anyone left alive?" he asked.

"Help us, mister," came a voice cracking with strain. "They done shot my ma and pa. Real bad."

Fargo rode closer and peered into the back of the wagon.

Under the flapping, torn canvas arch he saw a young man kneeling next to a man and woman. Both were covered with blood—their own.

He started to dismount but stopped when he saw movement from the corner of his eye. His hand flashed to his six-shooter and whipped it out. He had the gun cocked and aimed before he got a good look at his target. She was about the prettiest woman he had ever seen. In her early twenties, she was tall and dark-haired, with piercing blue eyes. There was a wild look he attributed to her brush with death, but it made her seem exotic, alive, and more vibrant than other women.

"A good thing you stopped, mister," she said. "He would have shot you." She pointed at a boy who was about old enough to start shaving standing at her side. He held a Greener goose gun in shaking hands.

"Doubt it," Fargo said, dismounting. "He didn't close the chamber properly."

"Joshua!" she said, exasperated. "You could have got us all killed!" She stamped her foot and looked lovelier than ever.

Fargo had to smile. "Don't be too hard on him, ma'am," he said. "Truth is, bluffing sometimes works better than gunplay. I don't think I winged any of the Apaches after my first couple shots, but firing in their direction was a good use of the ammunition. Joshua here might have helped just poking that shotgun out and showing them he had it."

"You saved us, mister," Joshua said, coming over. He held the long-barreled shotgun as if he had never seen it before. "Can you show me what's wrong?"

"You got another shotgun around?" Fargo asked, taking the goose gun from him and prying loose the shell jammed into the chamber. "This is the wrong size for this gun."

"Oh," was all Joshua said.

"Help them," came the plea from within the wagon. "They are both hurt bad."

"That's my other brother, Abel," the young woman said. "I'm Rachel Cleary."

"Pleased to make your acquaintance," Fargo said, touching the brim of his battered hat. "You'd better see to your folks. I'll check the other wagons, just to be sure." He doubted anyone had survived in either of the other wagons. The one that had broken down had received the brunt of the Apache attack, and the driver who had tried to outrun horse-mounted Apaches with a mule team was obviously dead. Fargo saw him dangling over the edge of the driver's box.

"I'll come with you," Joshua said.

"If you want," Fargo said, "but you can be of more use here. Help your brother and sister."

"We're doing what we can," Abel said sourly. "There's nothing he can do but mess up more."

"Tend the team," Fargo told the younger boy. "Get them ready for the trip back to Fort Stockton. That is where you set out from, isn't it?"

Joshua's head bobbed as if it were on a spring.

"But we're going to the town of La Limpia outside Fort Davis," Rachel complained. She poked her head out of the wagon. Her blouse was bloodstained, as were her hands.

"If I'm any judge," Fargo said, "your folks need a real doctor. Fort Stockton is closer."

Fargo retrieved a half dozen mules from the second wagon, but they were the only living things he found. The Apaches had shown their usual viciously efficient style of fighting and left everyone other than the Cleary family dead. Poking through the few remaining items in the back of the wagons showed nothing worth loading. Fargo returned with the mules and hitched them in front of the Cleary team.

"I can't drive this many mules," Abel said. Everything he did showed how he wanted to be rid of Skye Fargo. Fargo thought the young man might feel a tad guilty about the way his folks had been wounded while he had come through the attack without so much as a scratch. As the oldest of the menfolk left unwounded in the Cleary family, Abel was trying to take over.

That wasn't too smart. Fargo had spent his entire life on the frontier and knew how to stay alive. Abel and the rest of his family were obvious greenhorns blundering around and lucky not to have died with the rest.

"Do you have a bullwhip?" Fargo asked. Joshua handed him the fifteen-foot whip. Fargo unrolled it, then snapped it in the air. "Toss a rock, will you, Joshua?"

When the boy did, Fargo cracked the whip and sent the rock sailing like a bullet.

"Do that right over a mule's ear and you can get him moving mighty fast," Fargo said. "I'm not an expert mule skinner, but I'm better than you."

"I—" Abel began.

"Thank you, sir," Rachel cut in. "We accept your help." She turned and angrily whispered to her brother. Abel jerked away and went back into the wagon.

"You've all been through more'n you expected," Fargo said. "Don't be too hard on him. But I can get you back to Fort Stockton faster than you can move on your own."

Rachel's bright blue eyes fixed on him as she wrestled with the decision. The slow smile that came to her lips was a little sad, as if she didn't like surrendering her family to a stranger either, but also happy that he had come by.

"My name's Fargo, Skye Fargo," he introduced. "Excuse my lack of manners, but . . . ."

"But we've *all* been through more'n we expected,"

Rachel said, this time flashing him a genuine smile. She reached out and laid her hand on his for a fleeting moment. Then she turned and climbed into the wagon. She sat in the driver's box and stared down at him. "Well?" she asked. "When do we get rolling?"

SIGNET

★ THE TRAILSMAN ★

No other series has this much historical action!

❑ #194:	MONTANA STAGE	0-451-19384-9 / $4.99
❑ #195:	FORT RAVAGE CONSPIRACY	0-451-19247-8 / $4.99
❑ #196:	KANSAS CARNAGE	0-451-19385-7 / $4.99
❑ #202:	THE STALLION SEARCH	0-451-19503-5 / $4.99
❑ #206:	OREGON OUTRIDER	0-451-19581-7 / $4.99
❑ #208:	ARIZONA RENEGADES	0-451-19756-9 / $4.99
❑ #209:	TIMBER TERROR	0-451-19791-7 / $4.99
❑ #210:	THE BUSH LEAGUE	0-451-19684-8 / $4.99
❑ #211:	BADLANDS BLOODBATH	0-451-19694-5 / $4.99
❑ #212:	SIOUX STAMPEDE	0-451-19757-7 / $4.99
❑ #214:	TEXAS HELLION	0-451-19758-5 / $4.99
❑ #215:	DUET FOR SIX-GUNS	0-451-19866-2 / $4.99
❑ #216:	HIGH SIERRA HORROR	0-451-19860-3 / $4.99
❑ #217:	DAKOTA DECEPTION	0-451-19759-3 / $4.99
❑ #218:	PECOS BELLE BRIGADE	0-451-19891-3 / $4.99
❑ #219:	ARIZONA SILVER STRIKE	0-451-19932-4 / $4.99
❑ #220:	MONTANA GUN SHARPS	0-451-19964-2 / $4.99
❑ #221:	CALIFORNIA CRUSADER	0-451-19977-4 / $4.99
❑ #223:	IDAHO GHOST-TOWN	0-451-20024-1 / $4.99
❑ #224:	TEXAS TINHORNS	0-451-20041-1 / $4.99
❑ #225:	PRAIRIE FIRESTORM	0-451-20072-1 / $4.99
❑ #226:	NEBRASKA SLAYING GROUND	0-451-20097-7 / $4.99
❑ #227:	NAVAJO REVENGE	0-451-20133-7 / $4.99
❑ #228:	WYOMING WAR CRY	0-451-20148-5 / $4.99
❑ #229:	MANITOBA MARAUDERS	0-451-20164-7 / $4.99

Prices slightly higher in Canada

Payable by Visa, MC or AMEX only ($10.00 min.), No cash, checks or COD.
Shipping & handling: US/Can. $2.75 for one book, $1.00 for each add'l book;
Int'l $5.00 for one book, $1.00 for each add'l. Call (800) 788-6262 or
(201) 933-9292, fax (201) 896-8569 or mail your orders to:

Penguin Putnam Inc.   Bill my: ❑ Visa ❑ MasterCard ❑ Amex_____(expires)
P.O. Box 12289, Dept. B   Card#_____
Newark, NJ 07101-5289
Please allow 4-6 weeks for delivery.
Foreign and Canadian delivery 6-8 weeks. Signature _____

Bill to:
Name _____
Address_____ City _____
State/ZIP _____ Daytime Phone # _____
Ship to:
Name _____ Book Total $ _____
Address _____ Applicable Sales Tax $ _____
City _____ Postage & Handling $ _____
State/ZIP _____ Total Amount Due $ _____

This offer subject to change without notice.   Ad # N119 (8/00)

SIGNET BOOKS

Life can be a wild ride...sometimes
all you can do is just keep hanging on...

THE EXCITING NEW SERIES FROM MIKE FLANAGAN

RODEO RIDERS

☐ **#1 COWBOY UP!**   0-451-19883-2 / $6.99
Ex-rodeo champ Jack Lomas is a stubborn old rancher. He does things
only one way...his. A lifetime of hard work and regret has taught him
some tough lessons. But is it too late for this old dog to learn some new
tricks?

☐ **#2 RIGGED TO RIDE**   0-451-20033-0 / $5.99
Under the guidance of Lomas, young Clay Tory has risen in the rodeo
ranks. But the two are thrown like greenhorns when suspicious mishaps
befall Clay's opponents. Someone is trying to fix the contest in their favor
and get them out of the rodeo forever.

☐ **#3 FINAL RIDE**   0-451-20193-0 / $6.99
Sometimes, all you can do is keep holding on...that's top rodeo rider Clay
Tory's motto. But when personal tragedy strikes, Clay discovers how
much more there is at stake than just the glory and thrill of the win.

Prices slightly higher in Canada

Payable by Visa, MC or AMEX only ($10.00 min.), No cash, checks or COD.
Shipping & handling: US/Can. $2.75 for one book, $1.00 for each add'l book;
Int'l $5.00 for one book, $1.00 for each add'l. Call (800) 788-6262 or
(201) 933-9292, fax (201) 896-8569 or mail your orders to:

Penguin Putnam Inc.	Bill my: ☐ Visa ☐ MasterCard ☐ Amex_____(expires)
P.O. Box 12289, Dept. B	Card# _____
Newark, NJ 07101-5289	
Please allow 4-6 weeks for delivery.	
Foreign and Canadian delivery 6-8 weeks.	Signature _____

Bill to:
Name _____
Address_____ City _____
State/ZIP _____ Daytime Phone # _____
Ship to:
Name_____ Book Total $ _____
Address_____ Applicable Sales Tax $_____
City _____ Postage & Handling $_____
State/ZIP _____ Total Amount Due $ _____

This offer subject to change without notice.   Ad # N131 (9/00)